Enchanted Secrets

(Witches of Bayport)

By

Kristen Middleton

Copyright © 2013 by Kristen Middleton

Cover by
http://marintaniaart.weebly.com/

Cover Model

http://mihaela-vstock.deviantart.com/

Copyedited by Carolyn Pinard

carolynpinardconsults@gmail.com

The characters and events portrayed in this book are fictitious. Any similarity to real persons, living or dead, is coincidental and not intended by the author.

Copyright ©2012 by Kristen Middleton

All rights reserved.

No part of this book may be reproduced, or stored in a retrieval system or transmitted in any form or by any means, electronic, mechanical, photocopying, recording, or otherwise without express written permission of the author

Prologue

Salem, Oregon – 25 Years Earlier

"Wake up, girls," whispered mother, shaking her gently. "It's time to leave."

Adrianne's eyes snapped open and she smiled with giddiness.

Awake?

Who could sleep on a night like this?

The truth was, she'd been lying there wide awake and restless for most of the night, ever since mother had promised to take her and Vivian to the Moonlight Dance.

"Get dressed quickly," she ordered. "Make sure Vivian gets moving, too. And, please, don't either of you make a peep when you come downstairs."

Adrianne turned to her sister, who was still sleeping soundly on their double-bed. "Wake up," she whispered, squeezing her wrist.

"Leave me alone," moaned Vivian, slapping her hand away. "Can't you see... I'm dreaming?"

"Viv, mom's taking us to the Moonlight Dance, don't you remember?" she prodded.

Vivian sucked in her breath and opened her eyes. "Oh. I almost forgot. Did mother tell you it was time?"

Adrianne stood up and stretched her arms. "Yes. She also said that we have to move quickly and... not wake father."

Vivian, now fully awake and just as excited as Adrianne, threw away her comforter and scooted out of bed. "Well, what are you waiting for? We don't want to keep mother waiting or she might change her mind."

"Oh, Viv, I'm so excited!" gushed Adrianne, her blue eyes sparkling. "This is going to be the best night ever, I just know it."

"Let's hope so," said Vivian. "I hate getting out of bed when the sun hasn't yet risen."

"I know me, too. But this will definitely be worth it."

Both girls quickly removed their long cotton nightgowns and slipped into hooded robes made of crushed black velvet, with a red silk lining that felt cool against their bare skin.

"This robe feels strange and almost... sinful," said Adrianne. "I wonder if we should wear something underneath?"

Vivian shook her head. "No. Mother said not to wear *anything*. Not even our shoes."

Adrianne sighed. "At least there won't be any boys around. I'd simply die if one caught me dancing around with barely anything on."

"Oh, I don't know, I wouldn't mind dancing for Eric McDermott, even if I was in the nude," smiled Vivian wickedly. "He's pretty cute."

Adrianne's face turned red. They were only seventeen years old and Vivian sometimes said the most outlandish things. "Oh, my gosh, you'd really do that?"

Vivian tossed her long, red hair over her shoulder and ran her fingers through a couple of snarls. "Just for a few seconds," she said with a dark smile. "Then I'd turn him into a toad and toss him into the disgusting pond behind our house."

"Girls!" boomed a stern voice inside both of their heads.

Mother.

"Quit dawdling, girls. It's time to leave."

Adrianne and Vivian both squealed with excitement, and then padded down the old wooden staircase in bare feet.

"Quiet now," reminded mother, who held the front door open for them.

"Sorry," the girls whispered in unison as they brushed past her and stepped onto the cool wooden porch.

"Freezing," whispered Vivian, her breath visible in the brisk darkness.

Mother sighed and carefully closed the door behind the girls without making a sound. "Now, follow me quickly," she said, stepping off the porch and towards the back of the cabin where they were greeted by the crickets chirping away. Shivering, and not just from the brisk weather, she pulled the hood over her dark hair and glanced back towards the cabin one last time. Not seeing anything unusual, she released the breath she'd been holding and guided the girls towards the woods.

"This is so exciting," gushed Adrianne, following her mother into the forest. "I feel like I've been waiting for this dance forever."

"Forever has finally arrived, darling," answered mother. "And I promise you, this will be a night you'll always remember."

"I'm so cold," complained Vivian, her teeth chattering. "How far do we have to walk?"

"Actually, we're almost there," said mother, leading them towards a windy path that the girls had never seemed to notice before. "The fire will soon warm you."

It was the end of October and the air was crisp with the promise of an early winter. Adrianne didn't mind, however, she loved the snow. In fact, last winter she'd learned how to ice skate with her best friend, Rebecca, and they'd had so much fun laughing at each other as they'd slipped and fell on the ice. She wondered if she'd get to share this special occasion with her as well. As far as she knew, Rebecca had never been to the Moonlight Dance, either. "So, is Rebecca coming to this dance?"

Mother shrugged. "I really don't know. Just... please, remember not to talk about this with anyone at school or mention it to your father. He must never ever find out."

Yes, they'd heard it a hundred times already.

"But why?" asked Adrianne.

"Because, he just wouldn't understand," she replied softly. "You know how he is."

The girls were silent as they moved deeper into the woods. Soon they were met with the smell of burning cinder and the sounds from a crackling fire.

"Stop," said mother. She raised her thin, black wand and pointed it towards a large clearing straight ahead.

The girls watched in wonder as mother chanted a few words under her breath and the wand began to sparkle. Seconds later, the woods came to life.

"Oh, I see them," smiled Vivian, her eyes lighting up.

Where there had been nothing but dark trees and Evergreen bushes only moments before, now stood a roaring fire with several women congregating around it, all of them wearing the same matching black robes.

"Ah, Lisbeth," said an older woman, stepping towards them with piercing brown eyes and thin lips. "You've finally brought the twins, and on this Hallow's Eve when the moon is full... I don't think you could have chosen a better night for their induction."

Mother smiled proudly. "Yes, Meredith. It took some planning and patience, but I truly believe that they are ready for their initiation."

"Very well then, let's get everyone's attention," said Meredith. She then clapped her hands and the small crowd of women became silent.

"Excuse me," mother said, motioning towards the older woman. She smiled apologetically. "I'm sorry, Meredith, let me just speak to the girls for a moment. Please?"

Meredith nodded. "Of course."

"Come," said mother as she took both of their hands and pulled them away from the group. When they were out of earshot range, she turned to them and squeezed their hands tightly. She took a deep breath. "Look, I know that I told you that this was *just* a dance, however, it is *so* much more. You see, it is part of a ritual that every woman in our family has participated in, from generation to generation. Now, do not be frightened of the things you might hear or see this night, as I promise you, they won't hurt you." She looked at them and smiled proudly. "My lovelies, tonight you will be joining our coven circle and your powers… they will be magnified after this ceremony."

Vivian's eyes lit up. "Our powers will be stronger?"

Lisbeth smiled, her own eyes now glowing with excitement. "Oh yes, my dears. You are so special. Not only are you identical twins, but you are both *my* daughters, and there isn't one witch here," she said, glancing over their heads towards the others, "who is more powerful than me," she said, lowering her voice to a whisper, "even the High Priestess, Meredith."

"Lisbeth?" called Meredith. "It's time. Bring the girls to the circle."

The other witches had now formed a large circle around the fire and were watching the twins with an intensity that made Adrianne very nervous. She turned towards her mother to ask her what exactly was going to happen next, but the look on Lisbeth's face hushed her. It was a look of pure happiness.

"Come," she said, smiling lovingly at her two girls as she pulled them towards the other ten women.

Now the circle was complete with thirteen cloaked witches. Meredith smiled in satisfaction and then cleared her throat. "We are here to celebrate Samhain on this Hallow's

Eve. This is the time of beginnings and endings. We ask the blessings of the Wise Ones who guard the Portals of the World."

Adrianne listened half-heartedly to Meredith's words as she rattled on about the wind and storms, but wondered when they'd actually get to dance around the fire and where the music would come from. She loved music and dancing, which their father never allowed in their house. He was a minister, and a very strict one at that.

When Meredith was finished with her incantations, she raised her hands up to the sky and asked everyone to remove their robes.

"Oh... but I can't," exclaimed Adrianne, her cheeks flaming. "I'll be totally naked."

Her mother sighed. "Everyone will be naked, honey. It's okay. You're among friends."

Then Adrianne watched with shock as all of the women removed their robes, including their mother.

"Don't be such a prude," snorted Vivian as she discarded her own robe and stood proudly. "We're obviously both very beautiful and have nothing to be ashamed of."

She bit her lower lip. "But..."

"You have to do this, Adrianne," demanded Lisbeth in a tight voice. "It is part of the ritual."

Adrianne felt confused and ashamed as she dropped her robe to the ground. She stared towards the fire, fighting an intense urge to cover herself with both hands.

Noticing her modesty, Meredith smiled in amusement and continued with the ceremony. "We will now ask Goddess Diana to accept her new children into our coven. Protect them and keep them safe from those who do not understand, from those who can only hate. Give them strength and power to defeat their enemies and heal their loved ones, whenever it is needed."

Adrianne frowned. She knew she had special powers that she was supposed to keep from her father, but she also believed in God. Who was this Goddess Diana? Wasn't it blasphemy to pray to her? This was all so confusing.

Sudden gunshots echoed in the darkness, startling everyone. Someone screamed in pain and Adrianne watched as all of the women began to scatter into other parts of the woods, their pale bodies glowing in the moonlight.

"Girls, follow me!" demanded Lisbeth, grabbing her robe. "Hurry!"

Vivian and Adrianne quickly snatched up their cloaks and followed their mother while more gunfire exploded all around them. Just when they reached the ravine that would lead them back towards the safety of their cabin, Adrianne felt intense wave of dread and she could barely breathe. It was then that her mother stopped and turned towards the girls, her face as pale as the moon.

"Mother? Why are you stopping?" asked Vivian, looking around nervously.

Lisbeth didn't say anything, instead she crumbled to the ground. Both girls screamed in horror as blood began to spread across the top of their mother's robe.

"Mother!" cried Adrianne, dropping to her knees beside Lisbeth. She touched her cheek and began to cry. "No!"

"Devil worshipper!" growled their father as he sprang out of the woods with a shotgun clutched tightly in his hands. His dark eyes were filled with loathing as he stared at

Lisbeth's still body. "Now, *Witch*, you can spend eternity with *him!*"

Adrianne choked on her sobs as father raised his gun and aimed it at her this time.

"Daddy?!" she screamed.

He stared at her for a moment and then his eyes filled with tears. "I can't... I just can't, dear Lord," he moaned, falling to his knees. He held out his arm. "Adrianne... will you repent child... and seek God's forgiveness?"

Before Adrianne could respond, Vivian grabbed her wand, then closed her eyes and began to chant. It was then that Adrianne noticed the wand in her hand that was beginning to sparkle.

Mother's wand.

"What in Heaven's name are you doing, daughter?!" hollered their father, now raising the gun towards Vivian. "Put that down!"

Vivian stopped her chanting, pointed the wand towards their father, and whispered a single word. "Die."

His face turned white and then red. He dropped the gun and clutched his chest, staring at Vivian in anguish. "Viv, what have you done?"

Her eyes narrowed. "Die," she repeated, this time with much more venom.

Adrianne screamed in horror and ran towards their father, who now lay writhing on the ground, howling in horrendous pain. She kneeled down and took his hand. "Stop it!" she yelled, staring up at her sister. "You're killing him!"

Vivian smiled darkly. "That's the point."

Chapter One

(Now – 25 Years Later)

<u>Bayport, Michigan</u>

"Kendra, for the last time, wake up!" hollered my mother, who was now standing outside of the bedroom door, tapping her nails impatiently against the doorframe.

"Fine," I groaned, turning over. I looked at the clock – seven o'clock, and I only have twenty minutes to get ready. That was barely enough time to find clean underwear.

My sister flounced into the room, dressed in her new pink skinny jeans and white lace top. She plopped down next to me on my bed and shook me. "Get up, lazy bones! Aren't you excited? I just love the first day of school."

Summer was officially over and both Kala and I were starting twelfth grade. She was excited and I was resigned to the fact I still had nine more months of school before my "Great Escape." June couldn't get here fast enough.

"Yay," I mumbled, swinging my legs over the side of the bed. As always, she was a little too chipper for me to handle this early in the morning.

"So, what are you going to wear?" she asked, hopping off of the bed.

I yawned. "Um, clothes?"

Kala laughed and then started digging through our closet. She pulled out one of the new outfits my mom had chosen for me and held it out. Unlike both my mom and sister, I loathed shopping.

"Here, you should wear this purple hoodie with your white cargo pants," she said. "It's super cute."

I snorted. "Cute? Sure, on someone else."

My sister frowned. "Don't be so negative. It *does* look nice on you. In fact, if they would have had it in my size, I would have snatched it up in a heartbeat."

Kala, my skinny twin sister, never had to worry about clothes. Being a twig, everything always looks awesome on her.

"Fine, I'll wear it," I said, grabbing the outfit. I brushed past her to the small bathroom we shared and hoped I could still fit into the pants. Locking the door, I turned around and stared at my reflection in the mirror, wishing it was someone else – long brown hair, ghostly white skin, and blue eyes, which, actually... weren't half bad.

I sighed. *Who was I kidding? Nobody even noticed my eyes with this double chin.*

"Don't forget, we only have fifteen minutes," she called through the door. "I'll be downstairs in the kitchen."

Groaning, I quickly got ready, stuffing myself into the new clothes. When I finally got the zipper up, I stood sideways and groaned at the result. Although they were a size fourteen, they were much tighter than the last time I'd tried them on. Even the hoodie looked tight.

Crap.

Shuffling out of the bathroom, I grabbed a pair of sandals and looked longingly towards my soft bed, wishing I could just crawl back inside and veg out for the entire day.

"Hurry up, Kendra!" bellowed my mother's voice from downstairs.

"Hold your horses," I mumbled, wondering if I could talk her into online schooling.

God, that would be awesome.

Online, *nobody* would notice the thick roll of skin above my waistband or the way my legs jiggled when I moved too quickly. I'd be just another faceless student in pajamas, trying to finish up my senior year until I went to college, which to me, didn't seem quite as daunting. I'd never heard of any bullying in college, just stories about all of the crazy drunken parties and an occasional date rape.

Eh, come to think about it, online college was starting to sound more interesting, too.

Sighing, I decided to run the online idea by my mom later and went downstairs to the kitchen. I crossed my fingers, hoping that she'd made her famous chocolate-chip pancakes for our first day of school. It was an annual tradition.

"You look... nice," said my mom, who was a terrible liar. I could tell by the expression on her face that she also noticed the extra weight I'd put on in the last three weeks.

"We have to go," said Kala, grabbing her new designer clutch purse and a flaxseed granola bar. We'd both turned eighteen last month and she'd used her birthday money for the ridiculously priced purse, which I thought was gaudier than all hell. But, because of the French name imbedded on the inside of the thing, which nobody even saw, it was a 'must have' among many of the girls at our school. "I'll meet you outside."

"Take this," said my mom, handing me one of the flaxseed bars as I stared the bagels on the counter.

My eyebrows shot up. "Seriously, a *flaxseed* bar? This bird food isn't going to fill me up," I pouted. "Can't I just have a bagel instead?"

She brushed a few strands of her jet-black hair behind her ears. "Sidney's mom brought them over for the daycare kids and I don't have enough. I'm sorry, honey. You know they're loaded with carbs anyway," she said, leaning over and kissing my cheek. She's always trying to control my carb and fiber intake, which almost always leaves me hungry and unapproachable. It's one of the reasons I keep a stash of candy bars under my bed. Fortunately, my sister doesn't say anything about them. She'd rather let me eat than deal with my grumpiness from lack of sugar.

"Daycare kids," I mumbled, scowling at the granola bar. "They eat better than I do."

My mom runs a daycare in our home. Eight smelly little punks who've invaded our home and now there's never any peace. Since my dad died earlier last year, though, it's the only way my mom's been able to afford the house payments. She blames it on lack of college, and that's why she insists we both earn a degree.

"You eat very well, my dear," she answered with a wry smile. "Now, you'd better get moving before you miss your bus."

"Fine," I said, walking towards the door. "But if I can't concentrate this morning, it's probably because I'm trying not to poop."

She threw her head back and laughed. "What?"

"Yeah, mom... flaxseed... fiber... what are you trying to do to? Give me diarrhea?"

"Kendra, detoxifying your body is good for you!" she called as I shut the door behind me and stepped outside.

"Here it comes," said Kala, who was applying more lipstick to her already glossy ones.

The bus was just turning down our lane and we both rushed over to get to the bus stop across the street.

Our neighbor, John Frances, smiled at me as I stopped next to the curb. "What's wrong, out of breath?" He's our age and a total jerk. I despise him with a passion.

"Shut up, tool," snapped my sister, giving him a dirty look.

One thing I could say about my Kala was that she never thought twice about defending me.

I stabbed him viciously with my eyes and followed Kala onto the bus while everyone stared in shock at my sister. Kala *never* rode the bus. At least not last year, but that was because she'd been dating this superhot senior, Jamie Grant, who'd driven her to and from school every single day. Unfortunately, for Kala, he'd left for college two months ago and neither of us had our licenses yet, so it was the bus for the both of us.

"Sit here, Kala!" yelled Brandi, my sister's best friend.

Brandi was obviously still grounded from using her Mustang after sneaking out in the middle of the night last week. Apparently, she'd snuck to a concert that she'd been forbidden to go to, and her parents had busted her when she'd tried to get back into her window early the next morning. I didn't feel sorry for her, however. Brandi was blond with the perfect body and all the guys at school wanted to get into her pants, which I think most of them already had. Kala said she was a complete nympho and didn't hide that fact. In fact, she flaunted it with her short skirts and low-cut tops. The fact that my sister was friends with someone like that was a little unsettling, but I also knew that Kala held her virginity very sacred. More than once she'd told me she was saving it for Jamie, when he was finished with college and came back to put a ring on her finger. Only then would she let him go all the way with her.

Personally, I thought Jamie, who looked and dressed like a glamorized Ken-doll, was gay, and had been ecstatic to have someone like her for his girlfriend. She'd told me that he'd never pressured her to do anything as far as sex, and they'd barely kissed. Most of their time together was spent shopping or going to movies, and I'm not talking drive-ins. She'd mentioned it once to him and he'd stared at her in horror, complaining that the humidity would make his hair droop.

Yeah, if he was straight then I was definitely winning the next "America's Top Model" competition.

Kala went to the back of the bus and flopped down next to Brandi while I sat towards the front, as far away as I could from the others. I wasn't about to give anyone a chance to start teasing me during the first day of school. Last year had been bad enough. Apparently, being the pudgy sister of one of the most popular girls in school was hysterical to many.

I stared out the window and sighed, wishing that I would have stuck with the diet my mom had tried to put me on during the summer. But just like all the others, I'd cheated and then had finally given up. It was a horrible feeling, but what was even worse was looking at my sister, and knowing that if I'd lost weight, I'd be more like her – beautiful, confident, and able to wear "skinny jeans." Coincidently, most of my jeans already looked like "skinny jeans" on my thighs, but were supposed to be "relaxed fit."

That's why I hated to shop for clothes. Nothing fit like it was supposed to.

The bus made one last stop before it dropped us off at North Central High School, and we all stared at the person who stepped onboard. He was tall with longish, dark hair and a slender build. A fairly average looking guy, really, dressed in all black and wearing dark sunglasses.

"Vampire," somebody snickered from the back of the bus.

The "vampire" smirked and then stopped when he arrived at my seat. "Can I sit here?"

"Uh, sure," I said, staring up at him in surprise. When he sat down, I noticed right away that he smelled like vanilla, which was kind of odd, especially for a guy. I didn't mind, however, as it kind of reminded me of vanilla-bean ice cream or my mother's homemade sugar cookies.

He removed his sunglasses. "Hi, I'm Tyler."

"I'm Kendra," I said turning my face towards him.

"Nice to meet you."

My breath caught in my throat as our eyes locked. His were the most amazing shade of green I'd ever seen. They were so deep and hypnotic, I couldn't look away. In fact, I found it physically impossible to do anything but to try and stay afloat in those deep emerald pools. Just when I thought I was losing my mind, he turned his head and broke the spell.

"So, what grade are you in?" he asked, staring towards the front of the bus.

"Eleventh. I mean twelfth," I answered in a breathless whisper, still confused at what had just happened.

"Me, too," he said, smiling faintly.

I cleared my throat. "You're new to Bayport?"

"Yeah, my mother and I just moved here."

"Oh."

Okay, so I was no expert at conversations, especially with boys. Most guys avoided me like the plague anyway, unless they were trying to get closer to my "superstar" of a sister.

We didn't say anything to each other for the rest of the bus ride. When it finally rolled into the parking lot at school and the door opened, he stood up and moved back, allowing me to get out. He then followed me off of the bus and stayed next to me as we entered the school. When we got to the office, he stopped abruptly, and for some reason, so did I.

"Well," he said, replacing his sunglasses. "Maybe I'll see you in class?"

"Uh, sure," I said, still surprised that a cute guy like him was actually being nice to me.

"Good," he said, giving me a lazy smile that made my stomach flutter.

Chapter Two

My first class was "Homeroom" and I quickly sat down towards the back of the room.

"Hey, Kendra," said Amy, who I was semi-friends with. She sat down next to me and took off her eyeglasses, then proceeded to clean them with a small cloth.

"So, how was your summer?" I asked, relieved that I had at least one friend in Homeroom.

She plopped her glasses back on and smiled. "It was great! I went to band camp for a couple of weeks and learned some new songs."

Amy plays the clarinet, and that's all she talks about. I went over to her house one day last year after school, and she played "Somewhere Over the Rainbow" for me over and over. Now I can't even sit through the "The

Wizard of Oz" without wanting to throw the remote control at the television.

"Brenda!" squealed Amy, waving her hand in the air.

I also smiled at Brenda, who squeezed into the desk in front of me. Like me, she indulged in a little too much ice cream and pizza.

"Hi, guys," smiled Brenda, flashing a set of shiny new braces.

"Oh, wow," said Amy. "When did you get those?"

Brenda blushed. "During the summer. I have to wear them for a couple of years."

I nodded, smiling sheepishly. "I had my braces taken off last month. It was the highlight of the summer."

"Oh, I forgot that you even wore braces," said Amy, pushing her dark hair behind her ears.

"That's because nobody notices Kendra," snickered Mark Davis, who was sitting a couple desks away, "unless she's standing next to her hot sister with the perfect teeth."

It was true, for some reason Kala hadn't needed braces but my teeth had overlapped in the front so bad, I had to have them.

Some of the other kids laughed as he continued to mock me. I wanted to curl up into a ball and roll away. Instead, I looked down at my hands and wished that I could vaporize into thin air. I seriously hated Mark and all of his jock friends who picked on me whenever they were bored and wanted to look cool.

"Check out the new weirdo," said Mark with an ugly smirk. He turned his body back towards the front of the class and folded his arms across his chest. "He looks like something out of a cheap horror movie."

I looked up and my eyes locked with Tyler's – rather, his dark sunglasses. He was standing at the front of the class and scanning the room for a place to sit. There was a desk next to mine that was vacant, and for some reason, I really wanted him in it.

"What? It's too bright in here?" snorted Mark. "Nice shades, Dracula."

Of course, his friends only fueled his stupidity by laughing.

I glared at Mark, who was still chuckling at his own lame jokes, and wished I had the guts to tell him off; although, something in Tyler's expression told me that he didn't need any help from me.

Ignoring everyone else, Tyler removed his glasses and began walking towards me. Just when I thought he was going to sit at the desk next to mine, he took the seat behind me instead.

"Hey," he said as I turned around.

"Hey," I answered back, trying not to blush.

Some of the other girls in the classroom started checking him out, and soon were staring with glazed expressions, as if he was some kind of celebrity. I couldn't blame them, however. Not only was he cute, but his eyes were beautiful, magnetic, and more than a little... unnerving.

When the bell rang, the teacher, Mr. Henry, passed out the school's handbook and we spent a half hour going over each boring rule. No fighting, no swearing, no running, no guns, no tank tops, no pets, no gum, and last, but not least, no fun. My head was spinning by the time class was over and I was almost afraid to breathe, in case that was also against school policy.

"Bring a book to read tomorrow morning if you don't have homework," called Mr. Henry as we all shuffled out of the classroom.

I stepped into the hallway and started walking towards first period, which was my math class. I passed my sister along the way and she smiled at me.

"Is that your sister?"

I turned to find Tyler walking next to me again and felt more butterflies tickling my stomach. "Uh, yes."

"You must be twins?"

I nodded. "Yeah, but we don't look anything alike."

He smiled. "That's okay, being different is much more interesting."

I stared at him, wondering if he was from another planet.

"I don't know about that. Sometimes I'd rather be more like her," I said. "She's got it made and nobody gives her any crap."

He smiled. "She probably doesn't give anyone a chance to."

My eyes narrowed. "Well, I certainly don't *let* anyone give me crap, if that's what you're getting at."

"I never said you did. I was merely suggesting that confidence goes a long way."

He had me there. Every time I saw myself next to my sister, my confidence went out the door.

"So, um, where are you going?" I asked, nearing my classroom.

"Math," he answered. "We're in the same class. I hope you don't mind if I walk with you?"

How did he know what class I had next?

I blushed. "No, of course you can walk with me."

"Kendra has an admirer," snorted Mark behind us.

Tyler turned to him and smiled. "What's wrong, jealous because you don't have *any* admirers?"

Admirers?

My jaw dropped. Not only had he hinted that he was my admirer, but he'd also stood up to Mark, who was on the wrestling team and had muscles *on* his muscles.

Mark dropped his books on the ground, and then shoved Tyler, hard. "Why would I be jealous of a cow and her hoser boy-toy?"

Tyler removed his sunglasses and stared at him while several students gathered around anxiously to see what would happen next.

"Apologize for being an idiot," said Tyler evenly.

There were snickers and giggles from the crowd. Everyone knew Mark would go gangbusters on the new kid. What came next, however, surprised us all. The expression on Mark's face went from smug to friendly, almost to the point of being nerdy. "I'm sorry for being an idiot," he answered pleasantly.

"You'll never bother Kendra again," said Tyler.

"I will never bother Kendra again," answered Mark, still smiling at me like a guy who'd just met the girl of his dreams.

"Leave," said Tyler.

The next thing I knew, Mark turned around and began walking in the opposite direction.

Chapter Three

Stunned silence surrounded us as we all watched Mark walk away without hesitation.

This definitely had to be a dream, I thought. *No way would this happen in real life.*

"Disburse," mumbled Tyler. Then everyone suddenly came to life and scattered.

I watched in awe as Tyler put his sunglasses back on. "Uh, how did you do that?"

He smiled. "Let's just say, when I talk, people listen."

"*Are* you some kind of vampire or something?" I blurted out, the hair on the back of my neck standing straight up.

Tyler chuckled and shook his head. "No, I wouldn't be walking around during the day, now would I?"

"I don't know. That popular movie with the vampires and werewolves competing for the girl, all of those guys did just fine in the daylight."

He smiled. "That's fiction, Kendra. I can assure you that if I was a real vampire, I'd disintegrate as soon as my skin was exposed to the sun."

He was so matter-of-fact that I was afraid to ask him any more questions. Either he was completely bonkers, or I was. Or, it really was just one big, fat, crazy-assed dream.

Sighing to myself, I muddled these things through my mind as we walked into our math class and sat across from each other.

"My name is Ms. Byrd," said the teacher after calling the attendance. "I take this class very seriously, so there will be no talking when I'm talking, no passing notes around, and absolutely no cell phones allowed. If you have one, and I see it out of your pocket or purse, I will keep it until the end of the day."

This really irritated some of the other students who normally couldn't keep their hands off of their phones. It did nothing for me, however, as I didn't have a cell phone; my mom wouldn't even allow them in the house, which really sucked being a senior in high school.

"Also, no sunglasses," remarked Ms. Byrd, staring directly at Tyler.

He slipped them off, and I held my breath. When his eyes were exposed, the teacher paused for a moment, clearly unprepared for such an intense unveiling.

I smiled. It was really starting to amuse me – everyone's reaction to Tyler's piercing green eyes. It also took any unwanted attention off of me.

"Um, well then," she said, clearing her throat after regaining her composure. "Everyone, open your math books to page five."

During class, I noticed the teacher staring at Tyler curiously when she didn't think anyone was paying much attention. I also sensed, without a doubt, that he was very much aware of her interest.

When class was over, Tyler sprang out of his seat and took off without a second glance.

Sighing, I grabbed my stuff and followed the other students out the door, wondering if Tyler was actually going back to his home planet. The idea of him being an alien wasn't too far off the grid, especially with that mind control thing of his.

"Hey," said Tyler when I stepped out of the classroom.

I was surprised and slightly giddy to find him waiting for me in the hallway. His sunglasses were back and the warm vanilla scent engulfed me once again.

"Hey," I answered, biting my lip to keep from smiling like a dope.

Just then, Ms. Byrd stepped out of the classroom and looked like she was about to approach us, which for some reason, didn't seem to sit very well with him.

"Well," he said with a hint of irritation. "See you in English class."

"Uh, okay," I said, as he took off, obviously trying to avoid Ms. Byrd.

I glanced at the teacher and wondered why she'd freaked him out so much. She gave me a polite smile and then stepped back into the classroom without saying a word.

And how did he know we shared an English class at the end of the day?

I began to wonder if he'd somehow gotten ahold of my schedule.

"Is that your boyfriend?" asked Amy breathlessly. She'd been in the classroom, too, and had stared at Tyler for most of the hour.

I shook my head. "No, I just met him today."

"He's a little different, but... so cute," gushed Amy with a dreamy expression on her face as she walked away.

My next period was a health class and I had to sit at a table with three other students. I'd heard that we'd be starting a cooking series, and although I'd been really excited about it during the summer, when I saw who I was grouped with, my enthusiasm quickly died.

"Hi, Kendra," smiled Hailey Bates. She was also one of the most popular students in the eleventh grade as well as being one of the nastiest girls you could ever meet. Her cruelty to the other students was legendary.

"Hi," I said, praying she'd leave me alone.

When the other two students turned out to be two of her friends and basically just as evil, I wanted to shrivel up and float away. The class which had sounded so promising was quickly taking a nosedive.

"This must be your favorite class," remarked Hailey with a sly smile. "You get to cook and eat. Looks like you did a lot of that last summer."

The other girls started giggling but I ignored her, and instead stared at the teacher, who was beginning to take attendance.

During class we learned about the importance of using measuring scales for insuring a healthy, balanced diet.

"Obviously Kendra doesn't measure," whispered Hailey loud enough for me to hear.

The two other girls giggled again.

This time she really got to me and I don't even know why.

"Oh, someone's going to cry," she whispered, a triumphant look on her face.

My eyes burned as I tried to hold back the tears and I raised my hand to escape to the bathroom.

"Are you okay?" asked Miss Barnes, who seemed genuinely concerned.

I nodded without meeting her eyes but fortunately, she let me go.

The girl's bathroom appeared empty when I slammed through the door. I hurried into a stall and let myself go.

"Um, are you okay?" asked a soft voice in the next stall, surprising the crap out of me.

I cleared my throat. "Oh, I'm fine."

I wiped my face with a tissue and then flushed the toilet, trying to compose myself. When I opened the door and walked to the faucet to wash my hands, the girl from the next stall stepped out and our eyes met in the mirror. Her blond hair was pulled back in a tight ponytail and she was dressed in track pants and a hot pink T-shirt. She was also a heavier-set girl, like me.

"Hi," she said. "I'm Julie."

Embarrassed that I was caught crying, I smiled sheepishly. "I'm Kendra, sorry about the tears."

She snorted. "Are you kidding? It's not a big deal at all."

Although I'd never actually talked to her, I'd seen her in the halls laughing with her friends. She usually hung out with the brainiacs in the school and I'd heard she had the I.Q. of a genius.

"Still," I mumbled.

"Listen," she said, fumbling in her purse. "Everyone has their moments."

I nodded and watched as she applied some Chaptstick to her lips. "Maybe. I seem to have a lot these days and Hailey Bates isn't making it easier."

"Hailey?" she said. "Eh, don't let her get to you. She's going to have a rude awakening after she graduates, and someday, she'll regret being such a bitch to everyone."

"That's nine months away and I have her in my class for at least one semester," I mumbled, looking at my reflection in the mirror. "Sometimes I wish I could just drop out of school and be done with it."

"Don't," said Julie. "I know it sucks, but you can't let people like her win."

"They win no matter what," I said. "Popular girls are thin and pretty. They have nothing to worry about."

She turned to me. "Well, you can always lose weight but they'll still be ugly inside."

"I've tried and it hasn't helped me do anything but gain more weight from being depressed after I've failed."

"Well, don't give up. I lost twenty pounds last summer and I only have thirty more to go," she said with a proud smile. "It's hard work and takes a lot of willpower, but my old baggy jeans are proof that, yes, it can be done."

"I wish I had *your* willpower."

She sighed and wrote down something on a piece of paper. "You're standing in your own way of losing weight with that attitude. Look, here's my phone number. If you want a diet buddy to motivate you, give me a call." Then she handed me her phone number.

It was nice of her to offer, but I doubted that I'd ever call her. "Oh, well thanks."

"You're welcome," she answered with a smile. Then she grabbed her purse and left.

I stared at myself in the mirror again, and sighed. She was obviously right – I wanted to lose weight, but was putting up my own roadblocks. I just didn't know how to knock them down.

Chapter Four

During lunch I nonchalantly looked around for Tyler, but didn't see him anywhere in the cafeteria.

"Hey, sis," smiled Kala. She was sitting with the popular crowd when I walked by her table. "Want to sit with us?"

The other girls froze and stared at me in horror after that invitation. My sister didn't seem to notice, though, she just stared at me curiously.

I shook my head. "No, thanks," I said, hurrying away.

"Hey, Kendra," said Megan Fisher when I was about to walk past her table. She was sitting with three other girls, and all of them were dressed in black.

"Hi," I said, stopping next to them.

All four girls had a reputation for being a little strange. In fact, there were rumors that they practiced witchcraft and so almost everyone kept their distance.

"Saw you with that cute guy, the one with the sunglasses, today in the hall. When Mark was blowing smoke out of his pie-hole, *again*," said Megan.

I sighed. "Yes, as always he was being a total jerk."

"So what's with you and the new guy? Are you two seeing each other?"

I shook my head vehemently. "No, we were just walking to class together."

Megan looked at her friends and smiled. "Interesting. I might have to get to know t*hat* tall drink of water. Um, you don't mind, do you, Kendra?"

I shrugged. "No, why would I mind?"

"I just don't want to step on anyone's toes."

"You wouldn't be stepping on mine, don't worry." Although I had to admit, I did feel a spark of jealously.

"So, I'm having a get-together at my house after school. Would you be interested?" asked Megan in a low voice.

The fact that she was asking me over shocked me. Megan only lived a block away and we used to play together in the neighborhood when we were really young, but that had been years ago. Plus, I'd never seen the inside of her house. She was a nice girl, though, and I could always use new friends. "Maybe. I'll have to check with my mom when I get home. She may already have plans for me."

She smiled warmly. "Okay, I really hope you can make it."

Amy and Brenda were sitting together at a table in the back and they waved to me. I excused myself and walked over. I plunked down next to Amy and smiled. "Hey, guys."

"Hi. So what were the witches talking to you about?" asked Amy.

I smiled. "Come on, they're not witches."

"Maybe not, but they're still pretty creepy," said Brenda.

I glanced back over to Megan's table and none of them were talking to each other. In fact, they were all staring at me, which I had to admit, did kind of gave me the creeps.

"Okay, so they're a little different," I admitted. "Um, they invited me over to Megan's house after school."

Amy's jaw dropped. "Are you going to do it?"

I shrugged. "Maybe."

"You can't go over there," whispered Brenda. "I heard that Megan's mother is a real witch and has placed hexes on people."

"Oh, for Heaven's sake," I snorted. "There is no such thing as real witches."

Amy frowned. "Don't be naïve, Kendra. This whole town has a history of women performing witchcraft."

I raised my eyebrows. "Really?" We'd only lived in Bayport my entire life and I'd never heard anything about adults studying witchcraft in town.

Amy nodded. "Yeah, if you look up the town's history you'll find several articles written about the 'Witches of Bayport'."

Brenda leaned forward. "I actually did a report last year on them. Many of the witches moved from Salem in the late sixteen hundreds to Bayport, Michigan to escape the persecutions. *Entire* families of witches moved here."

"So you're saying that many of the people living in this town are descendants of witches and warlocks?" I asked, smiling.

"Something like that. But most of them gave up their practices over time," said Brenda.

"Probably because they finally realized they didn't have any real magical powers," said Amy.

"Well, I have to admit, it is kind of interesting," I said. "I guess it also explains why Megan and her friends are so into witchcraft. It's just too bad they waste so much time on something that won't do them any good," I said.

"Not to change the subject or anything," said Amy. "But where's that cute guy you were walking with earlier, um… Tyler?"

My cheeks grew warm. "I don't know, probably trying to stay as far away from me as possible, now that he's been in the school for half the day."

"I saw him in the hall earlier," said Brenda. "He was arguing with some girl."

Now that was surprising.

"Really? He never mentioned anything about knowing anyone here," I said.

"Maybe he's making some enemies already," said Brenda.

"Well, he did almost get into a fight with Mark Davis," I said. "But Mark backed down."

"I heard about that," said Amy. "Mark actually walked away from a fight. That is totally weird."

I nodded, still wondering about the girl Tyler was arguing with. Maybe he had a girlfriend? He'd just moved into the city but that didn't mean he hadn't met anyone over the summer. I wasn't sure what to make of that, and although it was kind of a bummer, it really wasn't any of my business. He was just a guy who'd been nice to me. So what if he had amazing green eyes and smelled like cake? He was different and it was still cool.

I had two more classes before last period, and they dragged on. The truth was that I couldn't wait for last period to see Tyler again. At the end of the day, I hurried to English class and watched the door, hoping he'd sit near me again. When the bell rang and he didn't even show up for class, I seriously bummed out.

"No homework yet," warned the teacher, Mr. Kemp, when the bell rang at the end of the day. "But next week I'll have plenty lined up for you, so be ready."

I passed by my sister on the way to the bus and she pulled me aside.

"I'm catching a ride with Mark Davis," she said. "We're going to the library first and then he's going to bring me home."

I stared at her in horror. "Mark Davis?"

She smiled. "I know, right? Mark is *so* cute. I can't believe he's even interested in me."

My sister obviously wasn't even aware of how pretty she was. And as far as I was concerned, Mark was a real tool; even if he'd apologized for being a jerk earlier.

"He's only cute if you like assholes who like to torment people," I snapped.

"Seriously? He was super sweet in History class today. To everyone, even Bonnie Hanson."

That was a surprise, considering he used to pick on her all the time because of her height. She was less than five-feet tall and he used to rip on her all the time. Another reason why I hated him with a passion.

"Fine. Well, have fun," I said, walking away before I missed the bus and she talked him into giving me a ride too.

I got on the bus and was turning on my iPod, when someone sat down in front of me.

"Hey," said Tyler, sitting sideways so he could talk to me. As usual, he wore his shades.

"Hi," I said, removing my earphones. "You missed a very boring class last period."

Tyler smiled. "I actually like English, if you can believe it."

I wanted to ask him why he'd missed it then, but I didn't want him to think I was nosy.

"So, what are you doing after school?" he asked.

I raised my eyebrows – I'd never been asked that question from a guy. "I um, I don't know, why?"

He smiled. "You should stop by my mom's shop. She just opened it last week and there are some pretty cool things in there."

"Your mom owns her own store? What kind?"

He removed his sunglasses and his hypnotic eyes caught me off guard once again. "It's called 'Secrets' and it's filled with the wonders of the universe."

I stared in awe at his eyes, wondering if he wore some kind of colored contacts. "Wonders of the universe?"

He threw his head back and laughed. "No, I'm just messing with you. She sells aromatherapy, incense, oils, and a bunch of other stuff."

"Oh," I answered. "Well, that kind of sounds... interesting."

He nodded and put his sunglasses back on. "There's something for everyone. My mother has traveled the world to fill her store with all kinds of odds and ends. Anyway, you should stop by. It's right on Main Street."

I'd remembered seeing the new sign on one of the storefront windows. It was within walking distance from my house and I didn't think my mom would have a problem with it. If anything, she'd be happy I was getting outside to walk.

"I'll see if I can stop by later today," I said, unable to wipe the smile from my face. I couldn't help but feel a little nervous and totally excited at the same time.

The bus stopped at his stop and he stood up. "Sounds good. I'll be there all night. See you later, Kendra."

Chapter Five

"Where's your sister?" asked my mom the moment I walked through the door by myself.

"Oh, she's with this *poser* named Mark Davis."

"Stop running in the house," ordered my mom as two little girls chased each other out of the kitchen.

"Mom, I'm going into town. There's this new shop I want to check out," I said quickly.

My mom cocked an eyebrow. "You want to check out a new shop... interesting. What is it – a new bookstore?"

I loved reading books and that was usually the only type of store I visited without being dragged, kicking and screaming.

"I suppose there could be books there. It's called 'Secrets' and it's on Main Street."

My mom nodded. "Yes, I remember seeing it when I drove home from the market the other day. I'm not sure what they sell, but when you find out, let me know."

I nodded. "Okay, see you later."

"Whoa...you're not leaving yet, my dear," she said. "Make your bed first."

"Fine," I groaned, turning away.

"Hey, Kendra?"

"Yeah?"

"You never told me how your first day of school went."

I shrugged. "It was okay."

"Okay? Well I guess that's a whole lot better than last year's answer of, *'it sucked'*."

I smiled. "Last year really *did* suck, mom."

She chuckled. "So... what time is this *poser* bringing your sister home?"

"Later," I called, leaving the kitchen.

"Great, that tells me a lot..."

I ran upstairs to my bedroom and threw my bed together as quickly as possible.

"Kendra!" called my mother as I was about to walk out the door, fifteen minutes later.

"What?"

She walked over to me and handed me a bagel. "Here, I saved this for you."

It was a little stale and I'd lost my appetite, but I smiled anyway. "Thanks."

"Oh, I almost forgot." She reached into her pocket and handed me ten dollars. "Just in case you find something you like."

"Thanks, mom."

She kissed my forehead. "Hurry back and let me know all about the store. I'd come with you, but these parents won't be back until suppertime."

My mom was a shopaholic. If she could have found someone to watch all eight kids, I'm sure she would have come with me.

"I will," I said, walking out the front door.

It didn't take me long to walk into town and find Secrets, which had actually been a tobacco shop before. As I approached the building, I noticed that it had been freshly painted from its original mustard-yellow color to a bright white with purple shutters. In front of the shop was a mixture of exotic flowers planted in a large black pot that almost looked like a witch's cauldron, which I thought *was* pretty cool.

"Calm down, idiot," I mumbled to myself as my heart began to race. "He just invited you to check out his mom's store. He's much too cute to be interested in someone like you."

Taking a deep breath, I pushed through the entrance and into the dimly-lit store. It was cool inside and smelled strongly like vanilla incense, which made perfect sense.

"Welcome," said the woman behind the counter. She was tall with long, brownish-red hair and a friendly smile.

"Thanks," I said softly, stuffing my hands into my hoodie pockets.

I gazed around the store and noticed there were only a couple of other people inside, one of them old Mrs. Buchaard, who was in her seventies and a little creepy. She'd never seemed to like children much and had always kept to herself. Some of the kids in my neighborhood used to claim she was an old witch. I didn't really know one way or another and didn't really care.

"Is there something I can help you find?" asked the woman.

"Um, no," I said, walking towards some dragon figurines. "I'm just looking around."

She smiled warmly. "Well, if you need help, don't be afraid to ask."

I nodded and started wandering through the aisles. The shop wasn't anything like I'd expected. There were large bookshelves and glass cases throughout that held everything from candles and colorful crystals to books that appeared to be hundreds of years old. It almost felt like an antique shop, without the usual junk.

"I have some lovely handmade jewelry in the front of the store," said the storeowner, suddenly standing next to me. She smiled again and I knew at once where Tyler had gotten his vibrant green eyes, although hers weren't quite as penetrating. "That is, if you're interested."

"I'll help her, mom," stated Tyler, coming out of the backroom wearing a different pair of dark sunglasses this time. In this dimly-lit store, I wondered how he could even see anything.

His mother studied me closely for a minute then went back behind the counter. "Okay, have fun."

"Hi," he said, standing over me. He seemed taller and even more mysterious in the shadows of the store.

I licked my lips. "Hi."

"Find anything interesting that you just have to have?" he asked.

Besides him?

I just smiled. "I don't know, I really just got here."

Then he surprised me by grabbing my hand. "I'll show you around."

My heart was doing flip-flops in my chest at the feel of my hand in his warm one. I cleared my throat and grinned like an idiot. "Okay."

"So tell me, do you believe in witchcraft?" asked Tyler as he pulled me towards the back of the store.

Chapter Six

I stopped I my tracks and laughed. "Witchcraft? Like in casting spells and stuff? Let me think about that. Um... no."

"Why not?" he asked, a serious expression on his face.

I snatched my hand back. "Not you, too? Listen, witches aren't real and either is magic, so quit teasing me."

A slow smile spread across his face and he removed his glasses. "Everything is real, Kendra. It's what you believe in that brings it to life or lays it to rest."

His eyes were hypnotizing me again. "What are you doing to me?" I asked hoarsely. "Your eyes..."

"Oh, sorry," he answered, replacing his glasses.

I took a step backwards, feeling the hair stand up on the back of my neck. "Maybe I should just go."

He grabbed my left hand again and gave me a sheepish grin. "No, not yet, please. I have some really cool things to show you."

How could anyone resist that smile?

I nodded. "Well, alright."

He let out a sigh of relief. "Cool. Okay, this way," he said, pulling me towards the door to the backroom. "Back here is where the magic begins," he said all mysteriously.

My eyes widened in surprise when we entered another dimly-lit room. This massive area was closed off to the public but it had to be twice the size of the regular store, which seemed impossible. My eyes gazed around the room, which was filled with hundreds of different boxes and containers, in different stages of being unpacked.

"Oh," I said as a white cat pressed herself against my legs, purring. "Who is this?"

"That's Sicely," smiled Tyler. "She's my mother's cat."

"She's adorable," I said, petting her soft fur.

"Believe me, she knows it," he said.

The cat meowed and took off.

"We used to have a cat, but she disappeared last year," I said softly. My mother had cried for days.

"Sorry," he said.

"His name was Salem and mom had him for years. He was a little testy, but we still loved him."

"Cats are pretty cool. Um, sorry it's such a mess back here," he said, swatting at some cobwebs. "I've been trying to help her unpack everything, but as you can see, it's a lot of work."

"How can you have such a large warehouse back here?" I murmured looking around in wonder. "The shop doesn't seem this big on the outside."

His lips twisted into a sardonic grin. "Don't ever be deceived by what's on the outside."

I rolled my eyes. "Yeah, yeah...I know, *Looks are deceiving.*"

"More than you could ever imagine."

"You're so dramatic," I stated, walking around the room. "I keep waiting for a sinister laugh from out of nowhere, or a loud clap of thunder whenever you hit me with your idioms."

He burst out laughing. "Sorry, I drive my mom crazy, too."

Tyler was definitely an odd character. But he was also super cute and nice to me, so I didn't really care about his silly quirks.

"So, what did you want to show me?" I asked, trailing my finger along a dusty old book about crystals.

"Well, I was looking for it when you arrived but still haven't located it yet," he answered, pulling down a box from a metal storage shelf.

"Oh," I said, lifting up something that looked almost like a magic wand. "So, your mom collects some pretty interesting stuff." I began waving the stick around.

"No!" shouted Tyler, lifting is hands in the air. "Put that down, please, very slowly."

I giggled. "What? Am I going to conjure up something or make you suddenly disappear?"

He stepped towards me with a stern expression. "Give it here."

When I handed it to him, he let out ragged breath, then put it away in a glass case and locked it.

I stared at him in amusement. "You're kind of serious about this stuff, aren't you?"

His look was pensive. "You... have *no* idea."

"Oh, this is cool," I said, picking up an ornately designed owl. "I kind of like the stuff your mom's selling. It's really different."

He smiled and then grabbed another box. "There are a lot of cool things, just don't touch them unless you check with me first. I don't want you getting hurt."

I shrugged. "Fine."

"Is everything okay back here?" called his mother from the doorway.

"Oh, mom, I almost forgot, let me introduce you. This is Kendra."

"Hi, Kendra," smiled his mother. "My name is Rebecca."

"Hi," I answered. "I love the interesting things you have here."

"There are some great finds back here. Just be very careful how you handle them," she answered. "Some of these items can be dangerous if you don't know what you're doing."

I looked at Tyler. "Yes, I've already been warned."

"I'm watching her," said Tyler.

She smiled wryly. "You be careful, too, young man."

He snorted. "You don't have to worry about me."

The bells at the front entrance jingled and Rebecca excused herself.

"Your mom is very pretty," I said to Tyler.

"Yeah," he mumbled. "It gets her into trouble sometimes."

"What do you mean?" I asked.

"Let's just say she receives a lot of unwanted attention. And that's the last thing she needs, right now."

I snorted. "Why, is she running away from someone?"

He froze and turned to me, his expression unreadable. "What makes you ask that?"

I smiled. "Sorry, I was only joking. Lighten up."

He opened his mouth to say something but then seemed to change his mind.

"So," I said. "I'd better not stay too long. I can come by tomorrow if you still haven't found the thing you wanted to show me."

He crouched down and opened up another box. "To tell you the truth," he said, looking up at me, "it might take me awhile to find it in this mess."

I looked around. "I can imagine."

He stood up. "Here, I'll walk you out."

"Okay."

As I turned to walk away, I almost tripped over one of the open boxes. I knelt down and picked it up. "You might want to find a better spot for this box; it looks like you have some breakables here."

"Okay."

I glanced inside and noticed several colorful bottles with labels. I smiled as I read some of the bottles. "Oh, what are these? Magic potions?"

He moved beside me and picked up one of the bottles. "Promotes hair growth," he said, staring at the label.

I noticed a purple bottle labeled "Promotes Thinness", and grabbed it. "Wow, I wonder if your mom would sell me this."

He sighed. "You don't need that," he said. "You look good. These potions are too dangerous to mess around with anyway."

I laughed. "Magic potions? You really think these are magic?"

"Let's just say, I know they work. At least the ones I've used."

"Oh," I said, trying to hide my smile. "Which ones did you try?"

He grabbed a brown bottle and showed it to me. "See, this one kills trolls."

"So, are trying to tell me that you killed a troll?" I laughed.

He stood up straighter. "No, I killed three, in fact."

His expression was so serious that I began to wonder if he was a little too caught up in all of this witchcraft nonsense.

I took a step backwards. "Well, I suppose I'd better go."

He removed his sunglasses. "I'm sorry. I hope I didn't frighten you."

"No."

But he was definitely starting to freak me out.

"I'm just saying these little bottles work, and some of them are very dangerous. My mom will be the first to tell you."

"Well, if a little bottle like this can help me get thinner, it's worth checking out," I said, deciding to humor him and his belief about potions. I grabbed the purple bottle again.

He grabbed my wrist. "Seriously, Kendra... you don't need that bottle. It might actually make you *too* thin. Besides, you look perfectly fine the way that you are."

I was flattered that he thought I looked "fine", but the threat of looking too thin wasn't helping his case one bit. I smiled and pinched my fingers together. "Listen, I'll just try a little."

He frowned. "Don't play with these things, Kendra. They can be very dangerous. You heard what my mom said."

"Well, let's just go talk to her then," I answered, turning towards the exit leading to the shop. He followed me as I walked through the main store and towards the register, where his mother stood reading some kind of book about "enchantments."

"Hey, mom."

"Hi," she said, putting the large book down. She looked at the bottle in my hand.

"Did you find something that interests you, honey?"

"Yeah, I found this bottle and was wondering how much you'd sell it for?" I asked, holding it up.

She looked at the bottle and her face darkened. "Tyler," she said, turning towards him, "where did you find this?"

"It was in a box on the floor." His lips thinned. "Kendra actually found it."

Rebecca turned to me. "This potion isn't something to mess around with, young lady. It can get you into big trouble if not handled properly."

I smiled. "Okay, I'll be extra careful, I promise. Is it for sale?"

She sighed. "Although something tells me I'm going to regret this, I *will* sell it to you, but *only* if you promise to follow the directions exactly. We don't want you losing too much weight."

I nodded vehemently. I still didn't believe a small bottle of liquid would really make me thin, but I was really getting caught up in her sales technique. She was pretty darn good.

"I promise. I will follow your directions to a tee."

She stared into my eyes for a few seconds. "Okay, I'll write them down. If you have any... complications with the potion, though, call me immediately."

"What do you mean by complications?" I asked.

"Well, something more than the typical side effects. Tyler, could you go help that customer over there?" she said, pointing towards a young girl looking at charms.

"Sure," he said, leaving the counter.

I narrowed my eyes. "What kinds of side effects are typical?"

"Upset stomach, headaches, heartburn. Those are typical. But if there is anything else, call me."

"Okay, how much?"

"Well, how much do you have?" she asked.

I laughed. "Well, I have ten dollars."

"That's how much it is," she answered, holding out her hand.

I pulled out the money my mother had given me and she rang up the sale. She then wrapped the bottle in tissue paper and stared at me with concern. "I'm not sure why you want to do this; you're a lovely young girl."

I lowered my voice. "No offense, but you're thin and probably don't understand what it's like when you look like me."

Her eyes softened. "Listen, Kendra, you are a very pretty girl and I seriously don't think you need to lose weight," she said.

"Thank you, but I'm getting really tired of being teased at school about my weight," I whispered. "And if this bottle can help me, even a little…"

She sighed and pulled out a pen and paper. "Okay, fine. Kids are cruel, I get that. Just, follow these directions," she replied, writing them down. "And don't take any more than what this says."

"I will and… thanks."

She folded the up the directions and slid it into the bag. "You're welcome. Just remember to be *very* careful."

I nodded. "I will."

Smiling, she handed me the potion. "Well, it was nice meeting you. I hope you'll stop by after you've taken the potion, so I can see the results."

"I will, thanks," I said, feeling giddy.

Just then another customer looking at old books motioned for Rebecca. "Oh, I gotta go. Call the store if you need me for anything," she said, squeezing my shoulder as she walked away.

"Goodbye."

I waved to Tyler, who was still assisting the young girl, who was now gazing at him like he was some kind of celebrity. He excused himself and walked back over to me while she watched him with open adoration.

"Looks like you've made an admirer," I teased.

He turned back towards the girl, who blushed and looked away. He smiled and then turned to me. "So, my mom cautioned you about the potion?"

"Yeah and I'll be fine."

Sighing, he walked me to the door. "You know, I really wish you'd just believe it when I say you don't need to change. You look great now."

My cheeks turned crimson, all this talk about my weight was beginning to make me uncomfortable. "Um, well thanks. I guess I'd better get going. So, see you on the bus?"

He nodded. "Sure, see you tomorrow."

Who knows, maybe you'll see less of me by then, I thought with a little smile.

As I walked out of the store, I had this crazy feeling that I was being watched. I stopped and looked around, but didn't notice anyone paying me any mind.

"Enchanter," whispered a gentle breeze against my ear.

I turned towards the sound of the voice, but found myself still alone on the sidewalk.

"Witchhh..." the voice hissed into my other ear.

Okay, I'm going crazy, I thought, twisting back around again.

Nobody.

With my heart hammering in my chest, I clutched my bag tightly and hurried away.

Chapter Seven

I didn't slow down until I was about two blocks from home and I heard someone call my name.

I groaned.

Megan.

I'd forgotten all about her invitation.

She was sitting on her porch, drinking what appeared to be tall glass of lemonade. She smiled and waved me over.

"Hi. Where are the other girls?" I asked, climbing the old wooden steps.

"Oh, they left a while ago."

"Look, I'm sorry I'm late," I said. "I stopped by that new shop on Main Street, 'Secrets', and lost track of time."

"Oh, I totally understand. I've been there; it has some really cool things."

I nodded.

"You didn't happen to see Tyler there, did you?"

"Yes, actually, his mother owns that shop."

"Fascinating," she said, twirling a long black strand of hair around her finger. With her large chocolate eyes and perfect cheekbones, I knew I wouldn't have much of a chance against someone as pretty as her if she was setting her sights on Tyler.

"Um, so I only have a little while," I said, wanting to get off the subject of Tyler.

"Come on then," she said, waving me inside of her house, which, honestly, looked like it had been built in the eighteen hundreds and hadn't been painted or fixed up since then, either. It *was* kind of creepy-looking and I knew that some of the younger children in the neighborhood were frightened of it, saying that it looked haunted. To me, it just looked old and worn.

"You have a massive home," I said as we walked inside.

She smiled. "Yeah. We inherited this monstrosity from my grandmother. You can get lost inside of this place if you're not careful."

"I bet," I said. The house had to be over four thousand square feet. "You must have had fun playing hide-and-seek here as a child."

Her eyes lit up. "Yeah, oh, my God, it was a blast! My cousins and I would hide and sometimes it would take over an hour to find someone."

I smiled. "Cool."

We walked through several candlelit rooms and I noticed that most of the furniture was covered with sheets, which I thought was kind of odd, since they were living in the house.

"It keeps the dust off," she remarked, noticing my confusion.

"Oh."

"You know, it's just me and my mother, unless we have guests, then she takes the sheets off."

"You don't have to explain anything to me," I said. "A big house like this, I totally understand."

"Yeah, it's a bitch to clean, too, especially that room," she said as we passed a small, cluttered library. "Thankfully I'm only responsible for my bedroom."

"This place is so big, it would take forever to dust and polish all of these floors," I stated, noticing that most of it was hardwood.

"Watch where you're walking," said Megan, as two cats raced by, chasing each other. "My mother has ten cats running around here somewhere."

"Hi there," I said to a tabby who'd brushed up against my leg before taking off to follow the other two cats.

"My room's upstairs," said Megan as we neared the staircase.

"So, um, where's your mom?" I asked.

"Oh, she's probably around… somewhere."

We went up the old winding stairway and down two more hallways until we finally reached her room. "Come on in," she said, opening the door with a secretive smile.

I gasped when I entered her bedroom; it was so different from the rest of the house.

She smiled at my shock. "I know, right?"

As I stepped onto her plush cream carpeting, I stared in awe at all of the modern décor in a room that was twice the size of mine. Basically, it was *the* coolest bedroom, I'd ever seen.

"Pottery Barn," she said, waving her hand in the air. "Gotta love them."

"This room is amazing," I said, staring at her large flat-screen television, which was bigger than the one in our living room. "I'm so jealous."

Even the walls were cool. One was the color of sapphire, and as I stepped closer, I noticed that someone had painted tiny, intricate stars that glittered almost... magically.

"Who painted your wall?" I asked, amazed at the details of each of each star.

"One of my aunts did it. Gemma, she's an artist."

"Awesome."

Next to that wall was an enormous platform bed with a velvety blue and black comforter. Plush pillows were scattered all over it, along with a black cat, who eyed me suspiciously.

"This is Willy," she said, motioning towards the cat. "He's mine."

"Hi, Willy," I said, offering a friendly smile.

He stood up, stretched his legs, and then jumped off the bed and pressed up against my legs.

She raised her eyebrows. "Wow, he likes you," she said. "He doesn't like *anyone.*"

I bent down and scratched his fur while he purred happily.

"I've got to get me one of those," I said, admiring the plush white leather chaise that sat next to her bedroom window.

"Go ahead, take her for a spin."

"Thanks," I said, sinking into the cool leather. I closed my eyes and smiled. "Oh, wow, this is freaken' amazing. I'm so jealous."

"Sometimes I fall asleep in it and don't wake up until the next morning."

"I bet."

Willy jumped on my lap and made himself at home.

"So," she said, staring at me as I pet her cat. "Did you find anything at *Secrets*?"

I shook my head. I wasn't about to tell her I'd purchased a bottle of potion to make myself thinner.

"Oh, that's too bad," she answered. "I've purchased quite a few items since they've opened."

"Oh?"

She nodded. "Yes, one must be prepared for anything, you know."

I wasn't sure what she meant but I agreed.

"I saw your sister with Mark today," she said, getting onto her bed. She lay on her stomach and rested her chin on her hands, watching me. "I was really surprised."

"I know. I can't stand him."

She nodded. "That was one of the reasons why I wanted to talk to you. Mark."

"Oh?"

Her eyes hardened. "He's dangerous."

"Dangerous?"

"He's into... witchcraft."

I laughed. "What is all of this talk of witchcraft today? It seems like everyone I talk to has something to say about it."

"You live in Bayport. What do you expect?"

"So," I said, watching her closely. "I heard that you're a witch."

I expected her to burst out laughing but she only shrugged. "Oh, who said that?"

"Some of the girls at school."

She rolled her eyes. "God, I hate gossipers."

"You and me both," I said.

She stared past me but didn't answer.

"So," I said, changing the subject. "Mark is dangerous, huh?"

"Definitely. He has a bad aura about him."

"What's an aura?"

"Basically, it's the energy he produces, and it's connected to his personality. Mark's is black. *Really* black."

"Oh," I said. "I'm assuming that's pretty bad."

"Yes," she said, sitting up. "So, if you care about your sister, keep her away from him."

There was a soft knock on the door. "Megan," called a woman's voice.

Megan rolled her eyes again. "What, mother?"

Megan's mother walked into the bedroom. She was an older version of Megan, but with permanent worry lines on her forehead. "Oh, I'm sorry; I didn't know you had a guest."

"Well," I said. "I really have to be leaving anyway."

"How's your mother doing?" asked Megan's mother.

"Um, good I guess," I said, surprised that she'd asked about her.

She smiled at me. "Could you please tell her that Adele says 'hello'?"

"Yeah, sure."

"Thank you."

I nodded and turned back to Megan. "I should probably get going now. It's getting late and my mom's going to get worried. Sorry I couldn't stay very long."

Megan stood up. "Another time maybe?"

I smiled. "Definitely."

She walked me back through the house to the front door and handed me something.

"It's my phone number," she said. "If you ever run into any problems with Mark, call me. Seriously."

"Uh, okay, thanks," I said.

She closed the door behind me, and as I walked away, I glanced back towards the house. Staring down at me from one of the windows above, was Adele. Before I could raise my hand to wave goodbye, she vanished into thin air.

I'm losing it, I thought, as I turned on my heel and walked home.

Chapter Eight

"Where've you been?" asked my sister as I walked in the door. It was almost six o'clock.

I shrugged. "I went shopping and then stopped at a friend's house."

She raised her eyebrows. "*You* went shopping?"

I nodded. "Yes. Enough about me, what's going on with you and Mark?"

Kala smiled. "I'm not sure yet. He's super sweet, though."

"He's as sweet as a moldy lemon," I muttered.

"Whatever," she said. "He invited me to a party this weekend and mom said I could go."

My jaw dropped. "A party? Really?"

"Um, yeah, she said it was fine – if you come with us."

I snorted. "Fat chance of that."

"Oh, please?" she pouted, following me as I walked towards our bedroom. "She seriously won't let me go if you don't come with us. Pretty please? I'll do anything."

"Kala, any party that Mark's going to will be trouble."

She scowled. "What do you mean?"

"Come on! You've heard the stories from last year. You know there's probably going to be alcohol and drugs. I heard Mark's a total lush."

"No, he doesn't drink anymore. I asked him."

I snorted. "Right..."

"Listen, if I don't go to this party, my friends will think I'm lame, and I'll never live it down. Please go with me? I will do anything, absolutely anything!"

I sighed.

"This could be good for you, too, Kendra! If people get to know you, they might be nicer to you at school. Come on, I've never asked you for anything."

She was right about that. My sister was always offering to do things for me and never asked for anything in return.

I owed her.

I sighed. "Fine, I'll go, but if anyone is rude to me or I see something I don't like at this party, we're leaving."

She squealed and gave me a hug. "Thank you! We are going to have such a blast!"

Something told me I'd be regretting this decision, but I bit my tongue and decided to hope for the best.

~~~

"So, how was your shopping experience?" asked my mom during dinner.

"It was okay," I answered. "I also stopped by Megan's on the way home and her mom Adele said to say 'hi'."

She raised her eyebrows. "Oh, okay."

"I didn't know you even knew Megan's mom."

"I really don't," she answered and then stood up. "Does anyone want seconds on the casserole?"

"Uh, no thanks, mom," I said, not really caring for the tofu surprise that night.

"Megan and her family are really weird," said Kala.

"Megan seemed pretty nice," I replied.

"Not very hungry tonight?" asked mom, pointing to my plate.

"Sorry," I said. "I'm just not into tofu, mom."

"It's so much healthier for you."

"Mom, it's gross," I said.

She turned to Kala. "So, you actually managed to talk your sister into going to this party, huh?"

Kala's eyes lit up. "Yes. I spoke to Mark and he's picking us up around seven on Saturday. I'm so pumped."

"Just make sure he gets you both home by midnight."

"Midnight?" pouted Kala. "Nobody leaves a party by midnight. Besides, we're eighteen now!"

"I don't care. Your curfew is midnight until you graduate, then you can stay out later."

"Fine," mumbled Kala.

"And I want to meet Mark before he brings you girls to this party."

Kala's face looked stricken. "Oh, God, mom. Don't make me drag him in here with all of the daycare stuff lying around. I'd die of total embarrassment if he walked into this place."

My mom frowned. "You shouldn't be embarrassed about my line of work. It's the only way we can keep this place. If he's turned off because of how or where you live, he's definitely not worth seeing."

Kala sighed. "Can't you just meet him outside? I'm sure he'll be in a hurry to get going, and it would only take a minute to talk to him anyway."

Her eyes narrowed. "We'll see. I'd rather him be the gentleman and come into the house to introduce himself."

"It's not the seventies or eighties, mom. Guys don't do that anymore."

"That's the problem," sighed my mom. "Nobody has manners anymore."

"Especially Mark," I said mumbled under my breath.

"What was that, Kendra?" mom asked.

"Nothing. Can I be excused?"

"Sure. Make sure you hit the sack earlier tonight so I don't have to drag you out of bed again tomorrow," she answered as I walked away from the dining room.

I hurried upstairs to my room and took out the bottle I'd purchased from "Secrets" and the note from Rebecca. The instructions said "one droplet only."

I carefully opened the bottle and squeezed some into the dropper she'd given me.

"Bottoms up," I whispered.

The potion was really bitter as it went down and I shuddered.

"What are you doing?" asked my sister, walking into the bedroom.

I quickly folded the bag up and stuck it into my nightstand. I grabbed a book about vampires from inside and shut the drawer. "Uh, just reading."

She fell onto her bed and began filing her nails. "Can you believe mom? I'm going to die if Mark comes in here. The kids have practically destroyed the inside of our house, and from what I hear, his parents are loaded. I'm sure *his* house is immaculate."

I wanted to scream at her... *who the heck cares what he thinks*! But I kept my cool. "So, there's a little crayon on the walls and some chipped wood," I said, opening up my book. "It's better than having to move somewhere smaller."

Truthfully, when my dad was still alive, the house had been kept up and in perfect condition. In fact, it had been my parents' dream home at one time. But that was before he'd died. My dad had owned his own construction company and my parents had designed and built the house exactly the way they'd wanted it. After he'd been diagnosed with cancer and had undergone many months of therapy without success, my mom had used what was left of his life insurance to pay off all the medical bills and then started doing daycare.

I miss you, daddy...

I tried to picture my father's face, with his dark hair and warm, loving eyes the same color as mine and Kala's, but it only made me long for him even more.

"You okay?" asked Kala.

I nodded, blinking back tears. "Yeah, just thinking about dad."

"I miss him, too," she said in a soft voice.

I knew that for the both of us, nights were the hardest, especially since he used to tuck us into bed, telling goofy stories, and using those corny voices of his. It had been a ritual, even as teenagers, and something we'd taken for granted until it was too late. Now, he'd been dead for only a year and a half, but it already seemed like a lifetime ago.

"I'm the luckiest man alive," he used to say. "Three beautiful angels, and they're all mine."

Now my dad was the angel and we were left with only pictures and bittersweet memories of him.

Life really sucked sometimes.

"I wish we had our licenses," mumbled Kala out of the blue. "Then we could just meet everyone at the party and I wouldn't have to worry about anything."

I nodded. "Yeah, but you need money to buy a car and you spend all of yours on clothing."

"I'm getting a job," she said, opening up her hot-pink nail polish.

I snorted. "Where?"

She began painting her toenails. "There are a couple of places in the mall that are hiring. I'm going to see if mom will drive me this weekend to fill out some applications."

I put my book down and stared at my pudgy toes, which hadn't shrunk one bit.

Potion, right.

I sighed. "Yeah, you know, I'd like a job, too, but there's no way I'm working in a clothing store or boutique."

"Why not? Then you can get discounts on clothing and stuff."

"I don't really care about clothes. You know that."

"Well, whatever. Maybe you can get a job at a bookstore or something. What about that shop you visited today? Are they hiring?"

An image of Tyler and I working together in the shop popped into my head and my heart fluttered. I closed my eyes and smiled. "I don't know, but I'm going to find out."

Chapter Nine

I woke up earlier the next morning; a little intrigued about what I'd find when I looked in the mirror. Unfortunately, the same lumpy body stared back at me. I closed my eyes and groaned.

Come on, what did you expect? There's no such thing as a magical potion to lose weight.

"What's wrong?" asked my sister, walking into the bathroom.

"Nothing," I sighed.

"Mom said it's going to be really hot today," she said, putting her dark hair up into a ponytail.

I pulled out a strappy sundress from the closet that hadn't looked too bad on me in the store and put it on.

Kala nodded in approval when she saw me dressed. "That looks good on you."

It was black with lime green and white dots.

"Thanks."

"Let me do your makeup?" asked Kala. "I'll make you look *gorgeous*," she drawled.

I bit the side of my lip. "I don't know. I usually don't wear makeup."

"I know but maybe you should live on the edge for once, sis. You have beautiful eyes. Why not accentuate them a little more?"

"Okay, but don't make it too obvious."

She smiled wickedly. "When I'm done with you, the guys will be hypnotized by your sultry eyes."

I smiled wryly. "I'd settle for them just shutting their mouths and leaving me alone."

"Believe me, when they see you, their mouths will be open and they'll be panting."

Right...

I sat down and closed my eyes, trying not to chicken out. When she was done applying some kind of grayish-blue shadow, dark liner, and mascara to my eyes, she squealed in delight. "Wow, you look pretty, girl."

I looked into the mirror and smiled. My eyes were definitely more... intense.

"It looks pretty good, thanks," I said, standing up.

"Pretty good? You look amazing!"

I didn't know about that, but I had to admit, I looked better than I would have thought.

~~~

When we sat down for breakfast, my mom eyed me curiously. "Wow, look at you all dazzling this morning. I don't think I've ever seen you with makeup."

I shrugged. "It was Kala's idea."

"Well, you look very pretty today. Your dress looks nice too, I'm glad I picked it out."

"Actually, *I* picked this one out," I said. "You didn't like the dots."

She smiled. "Well, I was wrong. The dots are working."

"Mom," said Kala. "Mark's driving me home again from school. We're stopping at the library again."

She narrowed her eyes. "What's with this new interest in the library? I didn't think you even liked to read."

Kala's face turned crimson. "Um, we are working on this project for school."

"You already have a project for school and have only been there for one day? What kind of project is it?" she asked.

"Oh, my God, look at the time," said Kala, pointing to the clock. "We're going to miss the bus if we don't leave now. I'll tell you about the project later, okay mom?"

"Sure. I can't wait to hear about it," she answered with a wry smile.

I followed my sister outside. "Project? Right. I'll bet you're creating your own little project in the back corner of the library."

Kala gave me a slow smile. "Actually, we were on the Internet. Mark was looking up stuff about mind control and witchcraft."

"Witchcraft? Did he say why?"

"No, he said it was for a project that *he* was working on. So, in all reality, we were working on a project together. I was just giving him... moral support."

I snorted. "Like he has morals."

She narrowed her eyes. "You really don't like him, do you?"

"He's a jerk, Kala. He picks on everyone, not just me."

"Well, I've never seen him say anything mean to anyone."

"That's because he puts on an act when you're around. He's a total *tool* otherwise, ask anyone."

She pursed her lips but didn't respond. The bus rounded the corner and we waited together for it in silence.

Chapter Ten

Tyler sat next to me on the bus. Today he was dressed in black chinos and a white polo shirt with the usual dark shades.

"What?" I asked, his gaze penetrating me right through his shades.

He smiled. "Nothing, just trying to figure out if my mom gave you the wrong potion."

My eyes narrowed. "What do you mean?"

"There's some kind of Makeup Potion, for witches without steady hands."

I laughed out loud. I wasn't sure which was funnier – the idea of a Makeup Potion or the fact that he spoke of witches as if they were real.

"It sounds funny, but you wouldn't believe how popular that potion is. And some of those witches need all the help they can get."

I was now laughing so hard, tears were forming. I was suddenly afraid my makeup would run, I held up my hand. "Okay, stop already with the Makeup Potion talk or I'm going to bleed eyeliner all over my cheeks and look scarier than any witch that you could imagine."

He bit back a smile. "Sorry."

"Anyway," I said, wiping a stray tear, "the Thinner Potion? It obviously didn't work."

Tyler sighed. "You didn't need it in the first place. You look fine."

"Well, not to most of the twelfth grade," I mumbled. "If I looked *fine*, they'd just leave me alone."

"Kendra, there are more important things in life other than worrying about how others view you," he said. "Anyone who makes fun of the way you look isn't worth trying to impress anyway."

"Easy for you to say," I mumbled. "You're in good shape and are too cute to worry about things like that."

Wow, did I just blurt that out?

He grinned. "You think I'm cute?"

My face turned red. "No, I mean... you blend in well with everyone."

"So, I'm *not* cute and I look like everyone else."

I groaned. "You are cute, okay? Quit teasing me."

He chuckled. "Sorry, I just couldn't resist."

"Did you ever find the item you wanted to show me in the store yesterday?" I asked, changing the subject.

His face became serious. "I did, actually."

"Where is it?"

"It's still at the shop. Can you come by after school again?"

"I think so. I'll check with my mom and see if it's okay."

"If you want, I can stop by and introduce myself."

I stared at him. "Really? You'd do that?"

He nodded. "It's probably a good idea, especially if we start hanging out and everything."

Hanging out? Did he mean as in dating or just friends? My mom's going to love this guy regardless, I thought.

I smiled. "Sure. That would be cool."

"Okay, I'll just get off the bus with you after school. Then we can walk to the shop afterwards."

"Isn't your mom going to be watching for you?"

"Nah."

"Okay."

When the bus pulled into the school parking lot, I was *so* giddy that Tyler was coming over. It might not be a date, but it was the closest I'd ever come to one.

Chapter Eleven

I went to the bathroom before first period and studied my reflection in the mirror. I was still amazed by the transformation that a little makeup had created. Luckily, it had weathered the tears Tyler had created with his potion talk.

"Wow, what's the special occasion?" asked Hailey Bates, stepping into the bathroom. She was with the two other girls from our health class. "Look at you... makeup and a new dress? Where'd they find the tent to make thing?"

The other two girls burst out laughing and I rushed out of the bathroom, feeling totally humiliated. I hurried through the hallway, my face streaked with mascara and tears, trying to ignore the smirks and giggles of the other students.

Damn, Hailey Bates.

I hated her more than anything at that moment, and all I wanted to do was escape and go home. As I made it to the exit at the back of the school, someone called my name.

"Kendra!"

Tyler.

I stopped and slowly turned around.

"What... what's wrong?" he asked walking towards me.

I shook my head as he got closer and tried to wipe away the tears with the back of my hand. "Um, nothing. Don't worry about it."

He removed his sunglasses and stared into my eyes. "Tell me what's wrong. Please."

I answered without hesitation. "Hailey Bates made fun of me and I lost control of my emotions." My voice sounded weird, almost robotic, even to myself.

His green eyes burned into mine. "She's an idiot. Do not allow yourself to feel belittled by her ignorance. You are beautiful, Kendra, inside and out."

A warm rush of pleasure spread throughout my body and I felt tingly all over. My heart lifted and I didn't care about Hailey's cruel words anymore. I smiled at him and sighed in relief.

He thought I was beautiful!

Tyler put his sunglasses on and took my hand in his. "Now, come with me."

~~~

"Where are we going?" I asked as he pulled me out of the school.

"It's a surprise."

My head was beginning to clear as I followed him through the football field. It had been fuzzy before, but now that I was breathing in the fresh air, my mind was racing with questions.

I stopped walking. "What exactly did you do to me back there, Tyler?"

He stopped and turned around. "What do you mean?"

"You know exactly what I mean. You did something to me with your eyes."

He shrugged. "Do you feel better?"

"Yeah, but that doesn't answer my question. What did you do to me, and why are you always wearing those dark sunglasses?"

"If I told you now, you'd think I was crazy. I'll explain it all later."

"I'm kind of thinking that I'm crazy right now for following you out of this school." I shook my head. "Especially after what just happened. God, I just know my mom is going to kill me."

He began to remove his glasses again.

"Stop that!" I hollered, pointing to his face. "Don't you dare do that thingy with your eyes again."

He pushed them back down and smiled. "What are you afraid of? Don't you trust me, Kendra?"

"That's just it! I don't know you enough to totally trust you. Just please, leave your glasses on."

"Fine."

I sighed. "So, where are we going?"

"Just a place I found recently. I think you'll like it. It's quiet and peaceful."

I actually did sort of trust him, but I wasn't even sure why. For all I knew, he could be taking me somewhere to slit my throat or take advantage of me. Of course, I wouldn't have minded the latter so much. He was cute and certainly had a way of making me feel good about myself.

As we walked away from the school grounds and into the nearby woods, I was amazed that nobody seemed to notice us leaving. Not even the gym class that had just stepped outside and onto the soccer field. Nobody even glanced in our direction.

"Here we are," he said, stopping abruptly.

I slammed into him and he steadied me. "Oh crap, I'm sorry," I said.

He let go of my elbow. "No problem. What do you think of this place?"

We were in the middle of the woods in a small clearing. "Well, it's certainly nice and peaceful."

He smiled and then surprised me by grabbing both of my hands. "You're not that impressed, I can tell. But, I want you to humor me for just a minute."

As long as he kept holding my hands, I'd humor him as much as he wanted. "Okay."

"Now, I need you to close your eyes, inhale, and take a deep breath of fresh air."

I nodded and then closed my eyes.

"Okay, now clear your mind and think of something that makes you truly happy, whether it's something from your past or present. Just remember to keep your eyes closed and concentrate. I'll tell you when you can open them back up."

"Okay."

"Don't forget to breathe," he said softly.

I inhaled the fresh air and tried to clear my mind, but all I kept thinking of was his warm hands holding mine.

"I'm going to release your hands," he said.

Rats.

"Kendra? Are you thinking of something that brings you joy?"

I thought about the half-gallon bucket of cookie-dough ice cream in the freezer at home and nodded.

"Make sure it's something that brings you pure happiness. I'm not talking about superficial things, either. Something you really wouldn't want to live without."

An image of my dad popped into my head and my chest tightened.

"Focus only on your happy memories. Clear your mind of everything else."

I thought about my dad and how he used to take my sister and me to the ice cream parlor on Main Street on Sundays. Just like me, he loved ice cream and used to order this gigantic bowl with endless toppings, one that could feed a dozen people. Then, all three of us would grab spoons and eat until we couldn't stand to look at the bowl anymore. It was a simple memory, but it was one I'd cherish forever.

"You're smiling, so it must be good," he said softly.

I nodded.

"Open your eyes."

When I opened my eyes, I didn't know exactly what to expect. Part of me had this fantasy that Tyler would somehow produce my father and he'd be holding out a giant bowl of ice cream.

"Wow...." I whispered in awe.

The woods appeared to be glowing iridescently and every color of flower, leaf, and rock seemed to be magnified. Even the grass under our feet seemed to sparkle.

"Watch," he murmured as a beautiful doe stepped through the woods and slowly edged towards us. Tyler held out his hand and the deer came close enough to nuzzle it.

"Wow, it's so beautiful," I whispered.

The doe looked at me with her honey-colored eyes and my breath caught in my throat. I could have sworn she was smiling at me.

Tyler removed his sunglasses and the doe turned to him. "Transform," he said.

A bright light surrounded the doe and I watched in stunned silence as it began to slowly change from a four-legged creature to one who stood on two legs

Tyler turned to stare at my reaction as a beautiful girl, her long blond hair glowing slightly as the light receded around her, stood before us. When I looked into her eyes, they stared back with the wisdom of someone much older than the teen standing before us.

"What?" I asked in disbelief. "What just happened? Am I dreaming?"

The girl chuckled and then curtsied. "Hello, my name is Trixie."

My head was spinning. "What are you?" I whispered.

She giggled again and clapped her hands. "I'm a Shape-shifter, silly."

Chapter Twelve

I must have fainted because the next thing I knew, they were both staring down at me and I was looking up at the clouds.

"Are you okay?" asked Tyler, grabbing my hand and helping me up.

I was a little dizzy and my mouth dry. "I think so," I croaked.

"I can't stay very long, Tyler," said Trixie, looking around anxiously. "Like I've told you before, it's really not safe here."

"Okay, Trix. Thanks for showing yourself to Kendra."

She nodded and then turned to me. "I'm so glad that they found you."

I put my hand on my chest. "Found me? What do you mean?"

Tyler smiled, sheepishly. "She doesn't know yet."

Trixie covered her mouth. "Oh, I'm sorry."

"What's going on here?" I asked, taking a step back. "What don't I know?"

"I'll explain everything tonight at my mother's shop. Right now, we'd better get you back to school."

My eyebrows shot up. "Do you really think I'll be able to get through this day normally after everything I've just witnessed here?"

"You're going to have to try, Kendra," said Tyler. "It's too dangerous to keep you out of school any longer, and you have to act like nothing's happened."

My eyebrows shot up. "Excuse me? Too dangerous? What in the heck are you talking about?"

Tyler grabbed both of my hands as Trixie slipped back into the woods. "Just like I showed you here, everything is not as it seems. There are others at school that can't be trusted. When we return, you have to act normal and don't tell anyone of the things I've shown you. Tonight, I *will* explain everything, and I promise you, it will make more sense. Just trust me, okay?"

"I... I guess. This is just so crazy. Tyler, seriously, I feel like I'm dreaming. Wait a second," I said, pulling away from him. "Is it that potion your mom sold me? Was it some kind of hallucinogen or something?"

"No, of course not," he answered, looking wounded.

I rubbed my forehead. "Okay. Fine. I'm sorry I said that, but you have to admit, this is some pretty intense stuff you're laying on me."

"I know."

I sighed. "So, what do we do now?"

"We need to finish out the day and then tonight, after school, I'll explain everything."

"Won't it be easier if you just told me now?"

He shook his head. "No. I have something to show you. It's the only way you'll truly believe what I have to say."

I mulled this over and nodded. "Okay. Well, then, let's go back to the school and get this day over with. I'm dying to find out what all of this is about."

He took my hand in his and led me back towards the school. When we reached the school grounds, I stared at the building and bit my lower lip. "I just hope we don't get detention for ditching class."

"Believe me, the teacher won't even notice we weren't in class when I'm done with him."

Sure enough, when we returned to the school, Tyler spoke to Mr. Henry in private for a couple seconds and the teacher seemed to have forgotten that we'd missed most of the class. We then snuck back to our seats with the other students watching in disbelief.

"Where did you go?" whispered Amy.

"Uh, left my homework at home," I mumbled, not wanting to get into it with her.

She motioned to Tyler. "What – and he left his home, too?"

"I don't know. We just arrived at the door at the same time," I whispered. "I don't know what's up with him."

When the bell rang at the end of class, several students got up and then did a double-take when they looked at me. It was then that I realized in horror that I had never bothered to check my makeup after crying. The mascara was probably smeared all over my face. I probably looked like a clown.

"I'll meet you in Math," I whispered to Tyler, who was also staring at me oddly.

"Uh, Kendra..."

"Math class!" I called back as I bolted out of the classroom.

When I stepped into the bathroom, I grabbed some paper towels and turned on the faucet, to dampen them. As I raised my head to look in the mirror, my jaw dropped.

"Oh, my God," I whispered, staring at my sister's reflection.

~~~

I was still trying to compose myself when the door opened and another girl walked into the bathroom. I looked up and recognized her from the bus.

"Hey, Kala," she said, reaching into her purse. She took out a tube of lipstick and put some on her lips.

I raised my hand and touched my face.

"Kala, you okay?"

Oh, God, she really thinks I'm Kala.

Our eyes met in the mirror. "Uh, yeah. I'm fine."

"You just looked a little pale there for a second," she said.

"I'm fine," I said, staring back into the mirror. There was no way that I could tell her who I really was; she'd never believe me.

The girl fluffed her hair and then turned to leave when she gasped in horror. "Oh, my God! Watch where you're walking, someone left a pair of underwear on the floor!"

When I looked down, I wanted to die of shame. The panties I'd been wearing had slid right off, and I hadn't even noticed.

"Oh, wow," I mumbled, my face bright red. I stepped away from them. "I can't believe that someone just *left* them here. Gross, huh?"

"Yeah," she said, scowling. "Very gross. Look, I'll catch you later."

"Yeah, later," I mumbled, picking the panties up as soon as she left the bathroom. I quickly tossed the underwear into the garbage can and then turned back to my reflection, still unable to believe what I was seeing.

"Kendra?" called Tyler, knocking softly on the door.

"I'll be out in a minute!" I called.

He opened the door.

My jaw dropped. "Tyler! What in the heck are you doing? This is the *girl's* bathroom."

He took off his sunglasses and stepped inside. "Right now, everyone thinks it's closed for repairs."

I took a deep breath and turned to face him. "Well, the potion worked."

He stared at me hard for a few seconds and then nodded. "It appears that way."

I turned back towards my reflection, still shocked that the thin person in the mirror wasn't Kala, but me. Funny thing was, I had mixed emotions.

"Uh, that dress is going to slide off soon if we don't do something about it."

I sighed. "Yeah, I need to go home and change. Can you get me out of the school unnoticed?"

"You're still asking me questions like that after everything you've seen?" he answered with a sly grin.

I licked my lips. "I guess I'm still trying to figure out if this is a dream."

He sighed. "It's not. Sorry."

I nodded.

"So, um, you don't seem very happy about losing the weight," he said, coming up behind me. "Isn't this what you wanted?"

"Yeah, but..."

He grabbed my hand and pulled me around, so that we were facing each other. "Kendra, you were perfectly fine before you took that potion. So you weren't a size two, who gives a crap?"

"Everyone –"

"Not me," he blurted, his cheeks turning slightly pink. "I didn't care. I thought you were pretty enough before."

This time, as his eyes burned into mine, my pulse went on overdrive, and I felt an overwhelming desire to press my lips to his.

"Are you doing something to me?" I whispered, as his vanilla scent washed over me.

"Like what?" he whispered back, his face moving closer.

"Making me want to... kiss you?" I squeaked.

He touched my cheek with his fingertips and I could barely breathe. "No. I'm not. Not this time."

I still wasn't sure if I believed him. "Could you... close your eyes for a second?"

His eyes twinkled in amusement but he did what I asked.

And nothing changed.

The butterflies were still whirling around in my stomach as if they were desperate to escape and I wanted nothing more than for him to like me the same way I liked him. I swallowed hard, staring at his lips, wondering what it would be like to kiss them.

"Kendra?"

My cheeks warmed. "Uh, okay. I guess this is all me," I admitted.

He opened his eyes. "It's *both* of us," he whispered, pulling me into his arms.

I closed my eyes and waited, hoping that he was about to do what it looked like he was about to do.

"Can I kiss you?" he murmured.

Please...

"Yes."

His lips were warm and soft as they pressed against mine. I slid my arms around his neck and pulled him closer, deepening our first kiss, which *had* to be the most amazing in the history of Bayport. It was sweeter than I could have ever imagined and I never wanted it to end.

"We have to go," he whispered, pulling away after a few more seconds. "Although, I never thought I'd enjoy being in the girl's bathroom this much."

I blushed.

He grabbed my hand and pulled me towards the door.

"How are we going to be able to skip the rest of the day without getting caught?" I asked.

"You forget who you're talking to," he said, smiling smugly. "I'll handle that part."

~~~

The halls were clear when we left the bathroom. Just when I thought we were in the clear, someone stopped us near the front exit.

"Excuse me?" snapped Ms. Johnson, one of the hall monitors. As usual, she looked very bitter about her career choice. "Where are you two going?"

Tyler removed his glasses and smiled. "We're going away. You can forget about seeing us."

The woman looked like a zombie. She nodded and walked away.

"Okay, how do you do that?" as we walked out the door.

He shrugged. "It's a gift."

"I guess," I said, laughing. "Is that why you're always wearing those sunglasses?"

"Partly, but the truth is that people are always staring at my eyes even when I'm not trying to do anything; it's a little unsettling."

"Well, your eyes are intense. But in a good way."

He smiled.

"So, Tyler, have you always had this 'gift'?"

"I have," he replied. "I'm an Enchanter."

I laughed. "What's an 'Enchanter'? It sounds like something from a Disney Movie."

"It's hard to explain. Let's just say I can manipulate people or things for special purposes."

I swallowed. "So, is that like magic?"

"In all honesty, yes, I do dabble in the art of magic."

"Oh."

He smiled wickedly. "Does that make you nervous?"

"No, for some insane reason, I feel really safe with you. It's just still hard for me to believe in magic."

He raised his arms in the air. "Magic is all around you, Kendra. When you open up your mind you will discover things far beyond your own imagination."

"Okay, Merlin," I answered, smiling wryly. "I'm starting to get the point."

A sudden screech of tires startled us both.

"Oh crap," mumbled Tyler, staring at the dark blue Volvo. "Here comes my mom. She doesn't look happy."

Chapter Thirteen

"What in the devil is going on?" asked Rebecca, as we slid into the backseat of her car.

"Um, let's just say Kendra took the potion we sold her, lost a little too much weight, and therefore, we had to leave."

"That's not what I'm talking about," she said, glancing back at him with a scowl.

He sighed and rubbed his forehead. "Well, dear mother, what *are* you talking about?"

"Do you not recall how I warned you to stay low? I specifically told you not to perform any kind of magic. That includes, ahem, 'Persuasion'. I heard from the grapevine that you've been using it quite a bit at school."

I wondered who the grapevine was but was too timid to ask.

He shrugged "Well, it needed to be done. Someone was hurting Kendra's feelings."

"I'm certainly proud of you for defending Kendra's honor. I just don't think it's very safe to be using your powers, especially right now."

Tyler didn't say anything, although I was dying to ask why it wasn't safe.

Rebecca changed the subject. "So," she said, smiling back at me. "You lost a little weight. Feel lighter on your toes?"

I snorted. "Actually, I feel as if this is all a dream."

She laughed. "Wait until we tell you the rest. You're going to feel like you're on another planet."

I folded my arms under my chest, which was also smaller, unfortunately. "Okay, you are *both* really freaking me out."

"Don't worry," said Rebecca. "It may seem freaky, but somehow, I know you can handle it."

I was glad she had faith in me, because I wasn't so sure of anything anymore.

~~~

Rebecca reopened the store and I followed Tyler into the back storage room again. For some reason the entire room seemed much more ominous than before.

"My mother wanted to explain everything to you, but I talked her into allowing me. She's not always very subtle, and truthfully, I'm better at these things."

"Forget being subtle, Tyler, just explain away," I said.

He pointed to my dress. "Are you sure you don't want to slip into something more... comfortable?"

I was definitely drowning in the dress.

I raised my arms. "I don't have anything to wear. Here or at home."

"Good thing you have a twin sister then."

"Won't help me at this moment," I said, pulling up one of my straps.

I thought about Kala, she was going to freak out. We were now more identical than ever before and I still wasn't sure how I felt about it.

"Wait, I have a better idea," said Tyler, removing his sunglasses. He furrowed his eyebrows and concentrated on my dress.

Within a few seconds, a shimmering light began to radiate from my dress and I watched in awe as it began to slowly shrink, until it hugged my body like a glove.

"Um, can you take it out, just a little?" I gasped. It was so tight; I thought it was going to rip with every breath I took.

His cheeks turned pink. "Sorry. My bad."

The dress loosened up a bit and I suddenly realized that he'd wanted it a little tighter.

I smiled wryly. "I guess you're not complaining about my new figure either."

Tyler's face turned serious. "You looked good before, Kendra. In fact, I think you're perfect at any weight. I thought I made myself clear on how I felt earlier."

I thought about our kiss and my heart felt like it was growing out of my chest.

I liked this Enchanter.

I liked him a lot.

And he didn't even have to put a spell on me.

Chapter Fourteen

"Um, so what is it that you wanted to show me?" I asked, clearing my throat. The electricity in the air between us and was intense.

"Oh, that's right," he said, putting on his sunglasses.

I pointed. "You don't have to wear those all the time, do you?"

He removed the sunglasses and folded them. "Sorry, I guess it's a habit."

"I just think it's probably good for your eyes to take them off now and then. You know, rest your peepers a little bit."

Okay, so that sounded kind of lame. The truth was, I really just wanted to see his dazzling eyes.

He smiled. "Well, I never really considered 'resting my peepers', unless I'm going to bed at night. But I'll take your advice."

I nodded. "It must be difficult to see indoors when you're wearing them anyway."

"Actually, I can see much better than the average person. In fact, I can see things others can't."

I crossed my arms over my chest. "Oh? You can't see through clothing, can you?"

"Do you really want to know?"

"Yes," I said. "I'd like to know if you can see…"

"What you're wearing underneath?" he asked with a wicked grin.

Then I remembered in horror that I wasn't wearing my panties and I quickly lowered my hands over my pelvis. He noticed this right away and raised his eyebrows.

"Tell me," I demanded, my cheeks burning.

"Fine, I can't tell what you're wearing under your clothing."

I released a sigh of relief.

"Unless, I try really hard," he said and then threw his head back and laughed when he saw my horrified expression.

I marched over and swatted him on the shoulder. "You are so… bad!"

"Ouch!" he laughed, again. "You wanted to know."

"Are you two okay back here?" murmured Rebecca, peeking through the door.

"Yes," said Tyler. "I was just going to find the picture."

Picture?

"Okay. I'll be out here if you need me," she said, walking away.

"I'll be right back," said Tyler, walking toward the back of the warehouse. "Don't touch *anything...* please."

I rolled my eyes. "Yes, you warned me yesterday."

I sat down on a metal chair and looked around the cluttered room, eyeing the boxes now with a new respect. Who knew what kind of magic was hidden in all of this cardboard?

"Okay," said Tyler. He was holding a five-by-seven picture frame but I couldn't see the picture. "I have something to show you and it's quite possible that you've seen it before. However, something tells me you haven't."

I took a deep breath. "Okay."

He handed me the picture frame and I stared at it in confusion. It was an older picture of two little girls, around five or six, and they were obviously twins.

"I don't understand," I said looking up at him.

"Look closely at the picture. Doesn't it remind you of someone?"

There was indeed something familiar about the girls. I couldn't quite place my finger on it.

"Look at the shape of their noses and the fullness of their lips. Ignore the color of their hair, she's obviously changed it. That's to be expected."

I nodded. Both girls had luxurious red hair. Their eyes were a dark blue with a catlike slant. "They're certainly cute," I said. Then something clicked and the blood rushed to my ears.

"Yes?" he asked, prodding me.

I looked at him in shock. "It's my mother!"

Tyler smiled. "Bingo."

I shook my head. "But she's not a twin. My mom told me that she was an only child."

He shrugged. "I would too if my twin sister was a ruthless and evil witch."

"Excuse me?"

"Your aunt Vivian and your mother are very powerful witches."

I stared at him for a few seconds and then burst out laughing.

His eyes narrowed. "Well, I'm glad you're amused, but it's the truth, and believe me, there's nothing funny about Vivian."

I wiped away the tears from my face. "Okay, that's enough. Quit messing with my mind, Tyler."

"He's not messing with you, at all," interrupted Rebecca, closing the door behind her. "Your mother is a twin and she's also a witch. I should know, we used to be best friends.

"I don't understand," I mumbled, looking at each of them, "My mom? You seriously expect me to believe that she's a witch?"

Rebecca smiled sadly and then pulled out another folding chair. She sat down next to me and looked at her son. "Tyler, go mind the store for a little while please."

He nodded and left us alone.

She reached over and took my hand in hers. "It's probably not my place to tell you this information, and I'm sure your mother will be furious when she finds out. But Tyler and I, well, we didn't have any other choice."

I stared into her eyes. "I just don't understand. Why would she hide all of this from us?"

Rebecca sighed. "Because of Vivian. Her sister is one of the most vicious sorceresses in the world. She's cruel, evil, and will stop at nothing to get what she wants."

A shiver went up my spine. "Well, what does she want?"

"She wants your mother's power all for herself. You see, when you're a witch and a twin one at that, it makes for a very powerful combination. In fact, when one of them dies, the other inherits the other's magic."

"And my mother's sister, my…aunt… wants her dead, so she can be more powerful?"

She nodded. "Vivian has been looking for your mother, Adrianne, for the last twenty years.

I raised my eyebrows. "Adrianne? My mother's name is Holly."

"Dear, Holly is your mother's middle name," said Rebecca, softly.

"Okay, this getting too deep for me," I said, standing up. "I need to go home and talk to her."

"Wait," said Rebecca. "I'm sure your mom has kept this from you and your sister, to keep you safe. It's very dangerous for all of you right now. Especially since..."

"What?"

The fear in her eyes made my pulse race. "Vivian knows your mom is here, in Bayport, and she'll do anything to find her, even if it means using you or your sister, Kala."

I bit the side of my lip. "You mean hurting me or Kala?"

She nodded. "Oh yes. If she finds you, she'll definitely use whatever means possible to hurt and destroy your mother."

"So, basically, we're all in danger?"

"Yes."

"How come you've found us, but she hasn't?"

She shrugged. "I'm sure your mother used a spell to keep her from locating you all these years."

"How does she know we're in Bayport?"

"Some spells get weaker over time. Or it could be that Vivian had help from someone else."

"So, is this why you moved here, to warn us?"

She nodded. "We'd hoped you were here, Adrianne once mentioned this place. She'd read about it and wanted to travel here. But I didn't know for sure until Tyler lucked out and found you at school."

I bit the side of my lip. "I know this sounds weird and I don't want to seem ungrateful, but why do you care so much? Why would you move here just to warn my mother about Vivian? Isn't it too dangerous to risk your own lives?"

She smiled. "Two reasons. Adrianne and I used to be best friends growing up. I do care what happens to her."

"And Vivian killed my father," interrupted Tyler from the doorway, his expression somber. "We need your mother's help to destroy her, once and for all."

Chapter Fifteen

"Are you okay?" asked Rebecca as I stumbled towards Tyler and the exit. I'd had enough of this magic talk, and just wanted to go home to my mom, so she could tell me that these people were crazy.

"Oh, I don't know," I answered thickly. "I've just shed thirty pounds, I witnessed a doe turn into a girl, and now I've been told my mother's a witch who's being hunted down by her evil twin sister. Seriously, I don't think I'll ever be okay again."

Tyler held up a bottle of water. "You don't look so good. Drink this, you're probably dehydrated from the potion."

"Good grief," said Rebecca, looking at her watch. "You two haven't had lunch yet. Tyler, take her to our house and feed the poor girl.

You can try and answer any more questions she may have, there, where it's safe."

He nodded. "Are you hungry?" he asked, holding out his arm to me.

I stared at him for a minute, trying to decide what to do. Food sounded like the only sane thing right now.

"Food will take the edge off of everything," he joked. "Seriously."

I sighed and slipped my arm through his. "Sure, but to tell you the truth, I'm pretty exhausted. I don't know if I can walk to your house."

"Who said anything about walking?" he asked with a sparkle in his eyes. He turned to his mother. "Um, it is okay if we teleport, isn't it? I know you said not to perform magic, but surely this is an exception?"

Rebecca stared at us for a minute and then nodded. "Okay, but just this once."

Tyler turned back to me and smiled. "You're in for a wonderful surprise."

"Swell," I mumbled, not really digging his surprises anymore.

He grabbed my hand and dragged me through the store, into their small public bathroom.

"Don't tell me... we're going to teleport through the toilet and end up at your house?" I asked dryly.

He shook his head. "No, silly... that's too gross. We're going to go through the drain."

I looked at the sink and studied the drain hole. It didn't appear any less gross or absurd. "Seriously?"

He burst out laughing. "No, I'm just messing with you."

I tightened my lips, not really in the mood for jokes. "Tyler..."

Sighing, he pulled me to him and circled his arms around my waist. "I'm sorry," he whispered into my hair. "I keep forgetting how new all of this is for you."

"It's okay," I said, inhaling his delicious smell, which seemed to comfort me somewhat. I looked up at him "Um, has anyone ever told you that you smell like vanilla bean ice cream?"

He smiled. "Hold onto me, tightly, and don't let go, for anything."

Although everything was crazy at the moment, being in his arms was better than anything I'd experienced in a long time. I certainly wasn't about to let him go. Not if I could help it.

Tyler closed his eyes and began chanting something under his breath. I shut my eyes, too, and held on as tight as I could, even when I felt his body temperature begin to rise at an alarming rate. Just when I thought I couldn't bear the heat radiating from him, there was a loud popping noise and I felt like we were being pushed through some type of spinning tunnel.

"Hurry, open your eyes," he said.

When I opened them I gasped in awe. Multiple colors of light, almost like a beautiful rainbow at the end of a storm, engulfed us as we moved through some type of twisting vortex.

"Wow..." I whispered, stunned by the beauty of the colors intertwining and bouncing off of each other.

He tightened his hold on me. "Almost there, get ready."

A second loud popping noise and we were pushed out of the traveling tunnel with such force that we both landed on plush, white carpeting, with me, lying right on top of him.

Chapter Sixteen

"Well, hello there," he said with a sly grin. "Come here often?"

I groaned and stood up.

"What?"

I shook my head and looked around in amazement. "So, this is your home?"

He stood up and smoothed down his shirt. "Yes, our humble abode. At least the one we feel the safest in."

I was surprised to find that they lived in such a contemporary-styled home. Since they were witches, I thought they'd live in something old and mysterious. This place was white, spacious, and from where I stood, appeared to have all of the modern luxuries.

"This place is beautiful," I said, looking up, admiring the tall vaulted ceilings and sky lights.

"Check out the view outside," said Tyler.

I walked over to a tall window that extended from the floor to the ceiling and looked out.

"Whoa, where in the world are we?"

"I told you it was a nice view," he smiled.

"A nice view? We're in the middle of nowhere."

Well we were somewhere, somewhere high up in the mountains and surrounded by snow.

"We're in Vail," he said. "It's a good place to hide. Vivian hates any kind of arctic weather."

My mother was the opposite. She dragged us skiing and ice skating every winter. My sister loved the cold months as well. I, on the other hand, didn't really care for winter. If it were my choice, I'd live in Florida all year long.

"So, you're hiding from her, too?"

He handed me a cup of cocoa, which seemed to have just appeared. He nodded. "Something like that, We moved here after she murdered my father."

I touched his hand. "I'm really sorry, Tyler," I said softly. "How did it happen?"

He sighed and then walked over to the white leather sectional facing the window. "I should probably start from the beginning," he said, sitting down. "My father worked for Vivian years ago, he was the head of her security."

"Security?" I snorted. "Why would she need bodyguards if she's so powerful?"

He scratched his chin. "Mostly for appearances. You see, she's also a famous pianist and doesn't always use her magic."

"Seriously?"

"Oh, yes. She's very vain about it, too," he said, his lips thinning. "I don't know if you've ever heard of Vivian Reynolds, but she's your aunt."

My eyebrows shot up. "Vivian Reynolds? Although I've never actually seen her, I know that my mother has some of her CDs. She doesn't listen to them, which I always thought was a little strange, in fact, they're actually still in the wrapping. Wow, I just can't believe that's her."

"She's probably too afraid to listen to them. Anyway, my dad worked for Vivian before he met my mother and then something happened. Something she didn't expect."

I leaned forward. "What?"

"Well, one night, Vivian paid my mother a visit and took my dad along with her, probably to try and scare her into telling her where Adrianne was. It didn't work. In fact, Vivian left in such a huff when my mother refused to tell her where Adrianne was that she demanded my dad go back that same night," his face darkened, "and kill her."

My eyes widened. "Vivian told your dad to murder Rebecca?"

"Yes. But my dad wasn't a killer. In fact, something drew my dad back to mom's shop, but it had nothing to do with murder."

I smiled. "Your mom is a very beautiful woman."

"Yes and she has a heart of gold. I'm sure that's what really drew my dad to her in the first place. Anyway, all I know is that he and my mother disappeared together that night."

"And Vivian freaked?"

"You could say that. I'm sure it's why she spent all of those years searching for them, as well as your mom. Obviously, she found my parents first and..." he looked down at his hands.

"Killed your dad," I said, softly.

He looked back up at me and his eyes were burned with hate. "She did and I'm not going to let her get away with it. I don't care if I die trying, I'm going to make sure she pays."

"I understand," I said, thinking of my father. If someone had killed him, I'm sure I'd feel the same way. "I just can't believe how evil that woman is," I said. "Thank goodness you and your mom survived. How long ago was this?"

"It happened almost two years ago," he said, his voice cracking. Embarrassed, he looked away.

"I'm so sorry, Tyler. I wish there was something I could do."

"There is," he said, standing up. He walked over to the window and put his hand on the glass. "Help us talk to your mother."

I moved closer and put a hand on his shoulder. "I will. I promise."

The snow began to fall and we both stared out of the window in silence, watching the flakes.

"It's amazingly beautiful here," I said.

He smiled. "I love it. You'll have to go skiing with me sometime."

"I'm not much of a skier," I snorted. "I suck, actually."

He grabbed my hand. "Maybe you just need the right guy to show you how to ski."

I smiled. A guy like him could make a girl forget all about the cold. "Maybe."

He bent down and kissed my lips, taking my breath away once again. "Kendra," he whispered, resting his forehead against mine.

I smiled. "Tyler."

He let out a ragged breath and stepped back. "I'd better watch myself. My mom would kill me if she knew..."

"Knew what?"

He smiled, darkly. "That I was kissing you when I was supposed to be feeding you."

"I won't tell."

He raised his eyebrow. "Are you flirting with me?"

Oh, my God, I was.

I put a hand over my mouth. "Yes, sorry."

He threw his head back and laughed. "What?"

"You just looked so flabbergasted there for a minute. Like flirting with me was so... horrific."

"No, I just don't want to be one of *those* kinds of girls."

"What do you mean 'those' kind of girls?"

I looked down. "You know – a tease."

"Listen," he said, tilting my chin back up. "You're unlike *any* girl that I've ever met." Then he brushed his lips against mine.

"Is that good or bad?" I whispered, when he pulled away.

He nodded. "Very good. Now," he stepped back and patted his stomach. "I'm starving. Let's eat"

"Okay. Um, one more thing, though – I was just wondering, did your dad have any special abilities?"

He smiled proudly. "My dad was also an Enchanter."

For some reason, his answer didn't comfort me one bit. "So he was a pretty powerful guy, but still couldn't beat Vivian?"

He sighed. "To tell you the truth, Vivian is already so fierce that if she finds your mother and steals her power, we're all doomed."

Chapter Seventeen

I followed Tyler to the kitchen and he grabbed a frozen pizza from the freezer.

"What, no magic involved in making lunch?" I teased, sitting down at the counter.

"You heard my mom, no more magic, except for the teleporting and maybe a cup of cocoa. So, until this thing with Vivian is over, I have to do almost everything the hard way," he answered as he removed the wrapper from the pizza. He licked his fingers. "You like pepperoni?"

I nodded. "So, why can't you perform magic? Will Vivian know?"

"The stronger the sorceress, the easier it to sense the energy created by magic, whether it's hers or someone else's."

"I hate to change the subject," I said, looking around the immaculate white tiled floor and marbled kitchen counters, "but your house isn't anything at all like I expected."

"What do you mean?"

"Well, your mom's a witch and you're an Enchanter, right?"

He nodded.

"Well, this place is so white and crisp; it's just too contemporary for a witch's pad. I'd have expected something more mystical and I don't know… old school, I guess? I mean, where's your herb garden for creating potions or steaming witch's cauldron? I haven't even seen a black cat or any pickle jars containing creepy things to make potions. I mean, come on!"

Tyler chuckled. "You really do read too many books."

"Maybe, but your mom's shop seems a little closer to what I'd expect to find under a witch's roof. This place, though, it's like something out of an architectural magazine, I'd never suspect the homeowners were… magical beings. More like yuppie interior designers or something."

He smirked. "Well, then we've covered are tracks pretty well. My mother didn't want to draw any unwanted attention. So this is kind of our hideout when things get bad."

"Well," I said, nodding, "if Vivian is aware of my family being in Bayport, then she'll find 'Secrets' blindfolded."

He shrugged. "It was a risk we had to take."

"Is your mom safe in the shop by herself?"

"She's used a spell for protection and we have some friends that are helping to keep any eye on things, just in case. She'll definitely know if Vivian is getting close."

"Friends...like Trixie?"

He nodded. "Like Trixie."

"Well, then I think it's time my mother knows you're here."

He let out a long, drawn-out sigh. "Believe me, she probably already does."

~~~

Tyler teleported us straight to my house after lunch. We landed on the floor in my bedroom, this time, with him on top of me.

"We have to quit meeting this way," he said, his eyes smoldering.

"Off," I said, pushing him away.

"Sorry, you just have this effect on me. Being a gentleman is getting harder by the minute," he said.

Pleased, I smiled. "Really?"

"Really, so let's get what we need from your bedroom and then find your mom."

I looked at my alarm clock and it was just after one o'clock in the afternoon.

"Okay. Turn around," I said, moving to my sister's underwear drawer.

He nodded and turned around.

I grabbed a pair of Kala's new panties and rushed to the bathroom. After slipping them on, I walked back into my bedroom and froze. "Do you hear that?" I whispered.

He shook his head and stared at me in alarm. "What's wrong?"

"It's too quiet,"

I walked out of the bedroom and he followed me downstairs. "Mom runs a daycare and nobody's around crying or screaming their head off."

The kitchen, which was usually stacked with dishes and chaotic children, was spotless and empty.

"Could she have taken the children outside?" he asked.

"I hope so."

We hurried to the backdoor and I opened it. The yard was filled with outdoor toys and the new jungle gym we'd recently installed. Other than that, it was also empty.

"Okay, this is weird," I said, stepping back inside. "Where in the world is she?"

He rubbed his chin. "Does she ever take the kids on field trips?"

"Sometimes, but she usually lets me and my sister know ahead of time, in case of an emergency."

"Then this *is* very bad. I think we should be prepared for the worst," he said.

I stared at him in horror as I realized what he was suggesting. "Do you think it's too late?" I asked in a strangled voice. "That maybe... Vivian's gotten to her?"

"I don't know," he said, avoiding my eyes.

A sudden knock at the door startled us and we both jumped.

"I'd better get that," I whispered.

"No, let me do it," he said, already heading towards the front door.

When we opened the door, a pretty blond woman stood beaming at us. "Oh, hello. My name is Michelle Evans and I was wondering if your mother is home? I sell Beauty Life Cosmetics."

"Um, no," I answered, eyeing the woman suspiciously. "She's not home, sorry."

"Oh, that's too bad," she said, pouting. "I spoke to her on the phone earlier and she told me she'd be here all day. She sounded really interested in trying our new line of lipsticks."

"We'll let her know you stopped by," said Tyler as he began to close the door.

Michelle stuck her foot in the doorway and her eyes narrowed. "Aren't you kids supposed to be in school?"

I cleared my throat. "Actually, we're homeschooled."

"Well, how nice," she said, studying my face. "Would you mind if I wait for your mother inside? It took me almost forty minutes to get here and she promised me she'd be around. Would it be okay if I just waited ten minutes?"

"No, I'm sorry. My mother is very adamant about not letting strangers into the house when she's not home."

Her lips curled into an ugly scowl. "Is that so?"

My breath caught in my throat when our eyes met. Not only were they the same color as my mother's, but they were now filled with such malice, that I instinctively took a step back.

"We'll let her know you stopped by," repeated Tyler firmly.

Michelle, who looked like she was going to explode just a moment ago, regained her composure and smiled sweetly at us. "Yes, of course. Well, I'm sorry to have bothered you. Have a nice afternoon."

As she turned away, Tyler shut the door and locked it quickly.

"What's happening?" I whispered. "Who was that?"

He looked at me. "That, my dear, was death knocking at your front door."

Chapter Eighteen

"We have to get out of here," stated Tyler, grabbing my hand and pulling me towards the backdoor. "She's going to be watching for your mother and we need to warn her before she gets back home. Do you have any idea where she might be?"

I shook my head. "Honestly, Tyler, I don't know. She's normally home right now. This just doesn't make any sense. Actually, nothing about today makes sense."

"Does she have a cell phone?"

I shook my head. "No, she says they give you brain cancer. She refuses to even allow them into our house."

Tyler nodded. "They are also an easy tracking device, probably the real reason she doesn't allow them."

Now that made much more sense.

"Is it possible that the school called my mom and she's there looking for me?"

"I guess it's possible. I did persuade the attendance clerk to forget about contacting your mother though."

I narrowed my eyes. "How did you do that when you were with me the entire time?"

"If I told you how, I'd have to kill you."

My eyes widened in shock.

He laughed. "No, I'm just messing with you."

I smacked him in the arm and then pushed him out the back door. "Let's go back to school, just in case she's waiting around there."

As we snuck away from the house towards the back alley, he looked up into the trees. "Vivian's probably watching us right now," he said in a low voice.

"From the trees?" I whispered in horror. I thought about how dangerous this woman was and it chilled me to the bone. Now, as I watched the wind blow the leaves around on the trees, everything seems so much more ominous.

"The birds, usually ravens or crows. She's been known to manipulate them to do her bidding."

I swallowed the lump in my throat and grabbed his hand. "I'm scared. I mean really freaking scared. Are you?"

He shrugged. "Nah. Whenever I encounter imminent danger, I try to concentrate on the solution, not the source."

"Well, have you found a solution for this problem yet?" I mumbled.

He stared at the sky. "Yes," he answered sucking in his breath. "Run!"

~~~

I'm not sure why he told me to run at that particular moment, but I wasn't about to argue with him. We both took off running down the alley.

"Hurry!" he barked when I stumbled over a break in the pavement.

"Trying!" I yelled back.

Just then hundreds of sharp "kraking" noises filled the air and I glanced behind us. "Oh, my God!" I shrieked in horror.

The sky was a blur of black, with thousands of birds screaming towards us, the sound of their wings flapping in the wind entwined with the roaring in my ears was deafening.

"Come on!" yelled Tyler, pulling me towards one of the neighbor's garages.

We crashed through the side door and I threw my arms around him. "Teleport us or whatever it is you do, right now!" I cried.

He nodded and began to chant.

"Going somewhere?"

I opened my eyes to find Michelle smiling coldly at us in the darkness of the garage, her blond hair now a vibrant red, her facial features totally changed. It was unnerving to see my mother's familiar, loving features twisted into a look of pure hatred.

"Please, don't hurt us," I whispered in horror.

She held up a wand and pointed it towards us, chanting some type of spell. Fortunately, however, Tyler had remained diligent in his incantations so we disappeared before she could finish.

Chapter Nineteen

We landed in the bathroom of "Secrets."

"That was close," I gasped, trying to stand up. My legs were trembling so much I thought they'd give out any minute.

He closed his eyes and released a ragged sigh. "You have no idea."

"So, did you recognize that spell she tried to use?"

He nodded. "Oh yeah, she almost annihilated us, both."

My eyes widened. "Wow. It's that easy, to kill someone?"

"With the right spell and sorceress, anything is possible."

The door opened suddenly and old Mrs. Buchaard stood staring at us curiously.

"Oh, I'm sorry, do you need to get in here?" asked Tyler.

She shook her head. "No, but you'd better get your butts moving if you're planning on helping Adrianne."

I stared at her in surprise. "What?"

She wagged her finger at us to follow her and said. "Let me introduce myself, I'm your mother's cousin, Clarice."

"What?" I repeated, this time in total shock. I glanced at Tyler who was smiling in amusement.

She grinned. "Oh, I know you weren't aware of it. We kept it from you and your sister for a reason. It was much too dangerous."

I stared at her and recognized some of my mother's traits. Cat-like eyes and high cheekbones. Otherwise Clarice's hair was completely white.

She patted her hair. "I know. I messed up a spell many years ago and it turned my hair white. I kind of liked it so... I kept it."

"Tyler!" called his mother, who was now rushing to close the shop. "What's happened? I've received some messages that there's been trouble."

"Trouble?" he snorted. "I'd say. Vivian showed up at Kendra's and we barely made it out of there."

She rushed over and threw her arms around Tyler. "Thank the stars above you're both safe. That woman is so unpredictable."

"The opposite of my mom, usually," I mumbled.

Rebecca turned to me. "I take it you didn't find her?"

I shook my head sadly. "No, we have no idea where she is."

"What about your sister?" asked Clarice, taking a step closer.

"Actually, I haven't spoken to her since this morning." I hadn't even considered how much danger my twin could be in.

"We'd better take a drive to the school and check on her then," said Clarice. "Quickly, before Vivian gets her mitts on her."

"Um, Kala's supposed to be getting a ride home with Mark Davis. They're going to the library after school to surf the Internet."

Clarice frowned. "Did you say "Mark Davis"?"

I nodded.

"I don't know. There's something about that boy that doesn't sit well with me," she said. "I've seen him around town, getting into all sorts of trouble. He's definitely not the type of boy your mother would want for Kala."

"He's a total jerk," I said. "I don't know how she can even stand to be near him."

Rebecca went behind the register and grabbed her purse. "Let's go find your sister, Kendra. If we're lucky, we'll locate your mother, too."

I sighed. "Can we drive by my house again, just in case she's there?"

"Of course, dear," answered Rebecca. She turned to Clarice who was digging around in her purse. "Are you coming?"

Clarice looked up. "Yes, I was just looking for my wand. It's got to be in here somewhere."

Rebecca opened up her own purse and held it away from her body. "Manifest," she said.

I watched in awe as a thin black magic wand shot out of Rebecca's leather handbag. It twirled in the air for a few seconds and then sat hovering in front of her face. She grabbed the wand and smiled at Clarice. "You may as well use magic now that Vivian's aware of our existence in town."

Clarice nodded and then held out her purse. "Manifest!" she ordered. Unfortunately nothing happened.

"Where is it?" asked Rebecca, stepping closer.

Clarice frowned. "Manifest!" she yelled. Still the wand did not appear.

"Is it possible that you left it at home?"

"I never leave home without my wand. It's just giving me a hard time. I think it's still angry that I hollered at it the other day."

"Oh," said Rebecca. "You have one of *those*."

"What do you mean?" I asked incredulously. "What… you hollered at your wand and now it's acting out?"

Clarice nodded. "Some wands are sensitive. Mine is very temperamental," she murmured.

"I heard that!" boomed a feminine voice from somewhere inside of Clarice's purse.

My jaw dropped as a long thin wand shot out of the purse and hovered close to Clarice's face. "Madame, you owe me an apology!" it announced.

"Well, I don't know about that," said Clarice, with a stiff upper lip. "You've been ignoring me all day. With Vivian around we have no time for such petty games."

"I'm not playing games! I'd just like a little respect, is all. I've served you for over fifty years, witch. Have you once ever asked me to perform a spell nicely?"

"Whatever do you mean?" she asked.

The wand snorted. "A simple 'thank you' or even a 'please' works wonders. Is that too much to ask?"

Clarice's eyes narrowed. "Fine. Thank you for all your magical assistance, I greatly appreciate it. Now get your petulant, bony butt into my fist before I turn you into a box of toothpicks!"

The wand immediately flew into Clarice's hand.

She smiled smugly and then looked at me. "You have to teach the wand who's in charge or they won't serve you properly. They like to test you from time to time. S*ome* more than others."

I was still flustered from seeing a wand talk, let alone think on its own. "Um, okay."

Clarice stepped closer to me. "You do realize you're a witch too, don't you, dear?"

"Me?" I asked, hoarsely.

"Oh yes. Your powers are dormant right now. But you and your sister have the genes to be very powerful witches."

Chapter Twenty

I chewed on what Clarice had told me on the way to the school but had a hard time really believing it. I was still trying to imagine my mother as a powerful sorceress. It just didn't seem logical. She changed diapers and served macaroni and cheese to children during the day. Did she really have the ability to teleport or put a hex on someone when she wasn't potty training?

"You okay?" asked Tyler, touching my knee.

"I think so," I said, staring at his hand.

"I know this whole thing is hard to grasp," he said, looking down, suddenly shy. He removed his hand. "Sorry."

I smiled. "You didn't hear me complaining."

He grinned and put his hand back on my knee.

"Tyler," warned Rebecca, who must also have eyes on the back of her head.

He removed his hand and smiled sheepishly.

I turned to look out the window as we pulled up to the high school. The last bell hadn't rung yet, so I knew we still had some time.

"Kendra and I should go into the school alone," said Tyler. "You ladies can keep a lookout for anything unusual on the outside."

"Just be careful," said Rebecca. "If you run into Vivian, send me a signal."

He nodded and we got out of the car.

"So, how *are* you going to let your mother know if Vivian's around?" I asked.

He pointed to his head. "If she opens her mind up, I can send her a telepathic message."

I sighed. "Oh, of course. I should have known."

The bell began to ring right as we entered the school and the sound of chaos soon filled the halls.

"I'm not even sure which class Kala has for final period," I said, as kids started rushing past us towards the exit.

"Maybe you should watch for her at this side of the building," he said. "I'll go to the other exit and keep an eye out."

"Okay."

I watched as Tyler put his sunglasses on and walked away. He seemed so much older and sophisticated than the guys sprinting past me on their way out of the school. Some of them were belching out loud or skateboarding towards the exits, and I began to wonder if Tyler was older than what he'd said. It was feasible since he only came to the school looking for us.

"Kala!" hollered Hailey coming straight towards me. She obviously had me confused with my sister.

"Hi," I said, gritting my teeth.

She looked down at my dress and grinned like a Cheshire cat. "Oh, I see they do make that dress in regular sizes. It certainly looks nice on you."

I forced a smile. "Well, thanks."

She nodded. "Too bad your sister can't lose all that extra weight. I'd have thought seeing you in the exact same dress would inspire her to eat less."

"Why are you so interested in my sister?" I snapped.

Hailey's eyes narrowed. "I'm not. It's just that I know you were talking about running for student council president and having a sister like her can't be good for your image. Maybe you shouldn't even waste your time running."

"What do you mean?"

She smiled cruelly. "Well, you're popular, of course, but she's pretty much in a class all by herself. Think about it, you'll lose a lot of votes and that would be totally humiliating. You could save yourself the embarrassment and just help someone else win."

I folded my arms under my chest. "Let me guess, you're running for president as well and would like me to back you up?"

Her face lit up. "You'd do that?"

I was speechless. Words just couldn't describe how much I despised Hailey at that particular moment, although, if I had the power to turn her into a toad right now, I'd turn myself into one instead. Then I'd turn her into a fly, so that I could devour her.

"Listen," she said. "Don't forget to meet us at 'The Pointe' after school. Mark mentioned that he was giving you a lift?"

The Pointe? That was a popular partying spot. I cleared my throat. "Oh, yeah. I'll see you later."

She stared at me curiously for a minute and then walked away.

~~~

As I continued to search for Kala, I noticed Tyler hurrying towards me.

"Did you see her anywhere?" I asked.

He nodded and then ran a hand through his hair. "I did, but unfortunately Mark hustled her out of the school so quickly, I didn't get a chance to talk to her."

I sighed. "Well, I know where they're going," I said. "The Pointe."

"What's "The Pointe"?

I smirked. "Exactly."

He snorted. "Do you know where it is?"

"I think so. There's a park a few blocks from here with a great view of the valley below. If you climb down the hill underneath it a few feet, you'll supposedly come to this hidden cave. That's where the kids hang out to drink or do whatever."

His eyebrows went up. "So you've been there before?"

I shook my head.

He looked a little relieved. "Let's go find it then," he said, taking my hand.

Chapter Twenty-One

"Clarice checked your house while you were inside and Adrianne is still not there," said Rebecca as we slid into the back of her car.

"Yes, I left her an encrypted note so she'd know you were safe, as well," said Clarice.

"Did you teleport from the car?" I asked.

"No," she answered, patting the outside of her purse. "I flew on my broom."

My jaw dropped. "You actually flew on a broom and now it's in your purse?"

She smiled weakly. "I just can't teleport like I used to. The last time I landed, my knees were sore for a week."

"But, seriously, you can fly on a real broom?" I asked. If I wasn't so worried about my sister and mom, I'd make her fly for me.

Clarice nodded. "Oh, yes. I find the old-fashioned way is much easier. Plus, I can see exactly where I'm going."

I sat back. "I wonder where my mother is? What if Vivian has already found her?"

"Your mother is not an easy witch to put down," said Clarice. "She's just as powerful as Vivian, remember. They're twins."

Rebecca sighed. "Yes, but Vivian practices Black magic, which Adrianne wouldn't touch."

"What's the difference?" I asked.

"Black magic is evil and it's used for one's own good. A witch who uses this type of magic learns how to control demons and spirits, using them for his or her own selfishness. Usually," Clarice added with a scowl, "to do harm to others."

"We don't dabble in Black magic," said Rebecca firmly. "It's dangerous and against our beliefs. Instead, we use only White, which works with the spirits," said Rebecca, "to heal others or create spells that help us defeat evil."

"Oh," I said. "Which is stronger?"

Rebecca and Clarice looked at each other.

"It depends on the witch and her inner strength," said Tyler. "If she believes she can conquer the other's magic, no matter what it is, she usually succeeds."

"So White magic doesn't always win?" I squeaked.

"Only if the witch knows what's she doing and believes her powers are the stronger of the two," said Tyler.

That revelation gave me goose bumps. I only hoped my mother's inner strength and beliefs were enough to keep her alive.

~~~

The park was crawling with high school students, most of them attempting to climb down the hill, many carrying small brown bags.

"Looks like a B.Y.O.B.," remarked Tyler.

"Bring your own broom?" asked Clarice. She smiled and her eyes lit up. "Oh, how wonderful. I used to enjoy those parties as a young girl, you know."

Rebecca laughed. "No Clarice, bottle, not broom."

Her smile fell. "Oh, those naughty kids."

"I can't believe my sister is going to this party," I said. "She told me Mark didn't drink alcohol."

"Hey, there they are," pointed Clarice.

Sure enough, my sister followed Mark towards the hill, although neither of them carried a bag of any sort. Kala didn't look very enthused.

"I'm going to talk to her," I said, opening up the car door.

"I'll come with," said Tyler.

"We'll keep an eye out for Vivian. She might be drawn to this kind of thing," said Rebecca.

Clarice raised her hands in the air and closed her eyes. "Yes, I can sense an aura of evil and deception radiating from some of these kids. This party screams of bad news."

"Sounds like a blast," answered Tyler with a humorless smile. "On that note, we'll be back as soon as we can."

We stepped away from the car and walked towards the edge of the hill.

"Hey, it's vampire boy," snickered Trevor Danes, coming up behind us. He was holding a two plastic bags filled with ice and plastic red cups.

I smirked. "Wow, Trevor, looks like you're all set."

Trevor was in our math class – a total surfer type of bonehead. He was also close friends with Mark.

He bobbed his head up and down. "You know it. Say," he said, motioning towards Tyler. "I didn't know you had a thing for bloodsucking-losers, Kala."

I opened up to let him have it when Tyler removed his sunglasses and motioned for me to remain silent.

"There goes the shades... hey, watch out for the burn, dude!" laughed Trevor.

Tyler looked into Trevor's vacant blue eyes. "Stay put, and keep an eye out for a woman with long, red hair. If you see her coming this way, howl like a wolf as loudly as you can."

Trevor's face became slack and he nodded.

I smiled. "Wow, I wish I could do that. Of course, I would have told him to drop dead."

"I don't know if that would work on a human," said Tyler with a straight face. "I've never attempted it."

"Oh, my God...I was kidding!"

He didn't say anything.

My eyes narrowed. "You mentioned something about trolls before. Um, was that real? Did you actually kill three trolls?"

"Yes, but they deserved it," he smiled. "They wouldn't let me over their bridge."

"Wow, you're amazing," I said, shaking my head.

"Sorry," he laughed. "I just couldn't resist."

I lowered my voice. "Seriously, though, are there really trolls?"

He pursed his lips and nodded. "Yes, and pray that you never meet one. They're nasty creatures and very hard to kill."

"Uh, okay."

We started climbing down the hill, which was actually steeper than I thought. "This would have to be very dangerous if you've been drinking," I noted.

"Yeah, look down below us."

There was a ravine at the very bottom of the hill, about three hundred feet down.

"If you didn't get hurt tumbling down, you might just drown in the ravine," I said.

Loud music and laughter blasted out of the large cave as we drew near.

"I wonder if the cops know about this place?"

"No," replied Mark, stepping out of the cave. "And I've worked hard to keep it that way."

I put my hands on my hips. "Where's Kala?"

His smile gave me the chills. "Come, I'll show you, *Kendra.*"

Tyler looked at me and I knew he felt it too. Mark was acting strange and he hadn't seemed surprised at all to see us.

Mark glanced at me. "Well, I have to say, Kendra, you're looking pretty hot. It's almost like," he said with a wicked grin. "Someone put a spell on you."

"Hey, Kala!" smiled Hailey. She was sitting with a couple of girls and drinking a beer. "I must be seeing things because I could have sworn you just passed by a few minutes ago."

I smirked. "Maybe you've just had too much to drink?"

"Not yet," she answered and then giggled.

"Don't worry, Hailey," smiled Mark. "I'll let you know tomorrow if you've taken off any clothes."

"Stop about the last time already!" she pouted. "You shouldn't have been looking anyway!"

I wasn't about to ask what she meant by that. Tyler just shook his head and removed his sunglasses.

We followed him deeper into the cave. It was getting darker and after a while, Mark pulled out a flashlight. "Watch out for spiders and other things lurking in the dark," he said. "You never know what you'll run into in these caves."

"Where is Kala?" I asked, getting worried. *Why would my sister be hanging out somewhere in the back of this smelly dank cave?*

Mark turned to me. "Don't worry, we're almost there."

We came to a tunnel and he motioned for us to keep following him.

"Are you sure she's back here?" I asked.

He turned back and gave me a reassuring smile. "Of course. Wait until we get there, you can see for yourself how great she's doing."

I shuddered at the way he said that, and even Tyler frowned.

"Here," said Mark, pointing towards a lit-up passageway. "Come on."

We followed him through the opening and my breath caught in my throat when I noticed my sister. "Kala?" I whispered in horror.

She lay on a giant slab of rock with her arms and legs tied together. Her eyes were closed and her skin was so pale, she appeared almost... dead.

"Oh, God!" I screamed, rushing towards her. "What have you done to my sister?"

"Wait!" yelled Tyler, as I slammed into some kind of invisible wall and fell backwards.

"So we meet again," chuckled Vivian, stepping out of the shadows of the cave. "Isn't this a quaint little family reunion?"

Chapter Twenty-Two

I stood up. "Let my sister go!"

"No," she sneered. "I don't think so."

With a very determined look, Tyler took a step towards Vivian.

"Freeze!" she demanded, raising her wand. "You try anything, boy, and I'll kill both girls."

Tyler clenched his fists. "Leave them alone. They're not who you're after."

"No, but they're good bait, don't you think?"

A bright flash of light lit up the cave and I sighed in relief when I saw Rebecca and Clarice appear, both of their wands raised.

"Teleport!" they cried in unison. Rebecca aimed her wand at me and Clarice aimed hers at Kala.

The next thing I knew, I was transported through the rainbow vortex and landed on my butt at Tyler and Rebecca's home in Vail.

"What happened?" moaned Kala, who was lying on the plush carpet a few feet away. She rubbed her temples and shuddered. "Man, I don't feel so good."

"Oh, my God, Kala," I cried, crawling over to her. "You're okay!"

Kala opened her eyes and gasped. "What... what happened to you?"

I smiled sheepishly. "I lost a little weight. It's a long story."

She looked around. "Where in the heck are we, and how'd we get here?"

"Um, we're at my friend Tyler's house."

She stood up and swayed. "Oh," she mumbled, touching her forehead. "I'm a little dizzy."

"Sit down," I said, motioning towards the white leather couch.

Kala stumbled towards the sofa and plopped down.

"Better?" I asked.

She sighed and put her head in her hands. "I don't understand, what happened?"

I took a deep breath and started telling her about mom and how she was a powerful witch.

"Excuse me?" she snapped, raising her head. "Are you on crack?"

"Listen, don't you remember being tied up in the cave? Or the crazy redhead who looked like our mother?"

She glanced at her wrists, which were slightly pink. "I don't remember being tied up, but I tell you what, I'm never going out with Mark again. He dragged me to that party and then left me alone in the middle of the cave."

I raised my eyebrows. "So you really don't remember anything else?"

She shook her head and frowned. "No."

Before I could say anything else, Tyler burst out of the vortex and landed on the carpet by her feet. Kala backed away from him on the sofa and began screaming.

I placed a hand on her shoulder. "It's okay, he's a friend."

"A friend...where did he come from? He wasn't here a second ago!"

"He just came from that cave party," I said. "Like us. We both teleported here as well."

She put her head back in her hands and moaned. "Okay, someone must have slipped me something in my diet soda. This must be what it's like to be stoned out of your mind."

"You're fine," I said, sitting down next to her. "Thank God."

Tyler cleared his throat. "So, are you two girls okay?"

"I think so," I said, turning to him. "Oh, my God, what happened to you?"

I had been focusing all of my attention on my sister and hadn't even noticed the horrible shape he was in. His clothes were ripped, he was sweating, and his hand was torn up and bleeding.

"I'm okay," he said. "A few scrapes from Vivian. Could have been a lot worse."

I frowned. "I think you need stitches. What in the heck did she do to you?"

"She blasted me with her wand when I went after her son."

"Her *son*?" I asked.

He nodded. "Yeah, you know, Mark.

"No way, seriously?"

He closed his eyes and let out a painful sigh. "Deadly serious, Kendra."

"Are you going to be okay?" I asked, seeing his face grow paler.

Before he could answer, Rebecca appeared out of nowhere.

"Is everyone okay?" she asked.

Kala's face was as white as a ghost. "I'm definitely losing my mind."

"Tyler's hand is pretty messed up, other than that, we're okay. Where's Clarice?"

"She went to go find your mother. Let me see your hand, Tyler."

He held out his hand and Rebecca pointed her wand. "Mend."

Kala and I watched in awe as the skin on his hand began to glow and repair itself. The next time I blinked, his hand looked smooth and free of any injury.

"Please tell me I'm dreaming," murmured Kala, "because if I'm not, I should be locked up.

"Oh, you're not dreaming," said Rebecca with a reassuring smile. "This is real and someday, you'll hone the same powers as your mother."

"It's true, Kala," I said. "Like I was trying to tell you, our mother's a witch. She also has an evil twin sister who practices Black magic and wants to destroy her."

She laughed, bitterly. "Really? So that she can rule the planet and kill us all."

"No," said Rebecca. "Just those who won't bow down to her every whim."

"Are you people out of your freaken' minds?" she yelled. "Our mother runs a daycare! There is no way she could possibly be a witch. That's absurd and I won't believe it for a minute!"

"Believe it, honey," murmured the soft voice of my mother as she began to materialize before our eyes. "Everything you've heard, it's... true."

Chapter Twenty-Three

"Mom!" I cried, stumbling towards her. "Where have you been?"

She raised both of her hands and took a step back. "Wait," she answered, breathlessly. "Please don't touch me. It's too dangerous."

"What? Are you hurt?" I asked, noticing how pale and delicate she looked.

She swayed slightly and blinked. "Vivian's... placed a spell on me." Then before I could say or do anything, she collapsed to the floor.

"Mom!" I sobbed, reaching for her.

"Wait! Stay back!" hollered Clarice, who suddenly materialized next to her. "You mustn't touch her!"

Rebecca placed herself between us and then turned to Clarice. "Take Adrianne into my bedroom."

She waved her wand. Then, they were both gone.

"What in God's name is wrong with our mother?" choked Kala, who was still sitting on the sofa. "And who *are* you people?"

Tyler removed his sunglasses and walked stepped forward. "Don't be afraid," he said softly.

She stared at him in confusion.

"You must relax and listen to your sister. She's telling you the truth. You need to be strong so you can help each other."

Kala's eyes were now dilated. She nodded her head slowly. "Yes."

Tyler, who also looked exhausted, turned to me. "Okay, now, talk to her."

"Kala?" I asked, edging back towards the sofa. "Are you okay?"

She turned to me and I watched as her eyes began to refocus. She nodded. "Yes. I'm just trying to absorb everything."

Rebecca stepped forward and squeezed her shoulder. Then, she looked at me. "I'll be right back. I'm going to find out what happened to your mother, although," she said with a pained expression, "I think it's pretty obvious."

"Listen," I said to Kala as soon as we were alone. "Everything I've told you is true. Vivian *is* mom's twin sister. She wants to kill her so she can steal all of her magic. I guess if you're a twin *and* a witch you can absorb the other one's magic after they die."

She turned to me in horror. "Why would her own sister want to do this, and secondly, why didn't mom ever tell us she was a witch with an evil twin sister?"

I sighed. "To protect us. The less we knew, the better."

Kala wiped the tears from her eyes. "This just seems so... crazy," she laughed bitterly. "I mean witches, spells, and... what about your friend Tyler?" her eyes grew large. "Is he a warlock?"

I shook my head. "No, he's an Enchanter. Tyler inherited his gifts from his father, who, by the way, was also killed by Vivian."

"Oh of course," she mumbled.

"Girls," said Clarice, coming up behind us.

We both shot up off of the couch.

She smiled sadly. "We must talk. Please sit down."

I sat back down next to my sister and cleared my throat. "So, is mom okay?" I asked.

Her face darkened. "Well, she's been hexed."

"What does that mean?" asked Kala.

"Vivian has put a curse on your mother."

Kala's lips began to tremble. "A curse? What do you mean? Is she going to die?"

Not one to mince words, she replied, "Yes she *will* die, unless we can stop the curse."

"Oh, my God!" I moaned. "She might really die? Seriously?"

"How can we stop it?" asked Kala, wiping her eyes. "There must be a way?"

"Vivian must die," stated Tyler, coming out of the kitchen. "The only way you can save your mother, is to destroy Vivian first."

~~~

"How in the world are we supposed to kill her? Wouldn't you have done it years ago if it was feasible?" I asked.

"We've never tried to actually *kill* her before," said Clarice. "To be honest, I'm not sure if we're even strong enough to do it."

"That's why we work together," said Tyler. "She has weaknesses. I know she does.

In fact, the Shape-shifters have been watching her for me."

"How clever, my dear boy. Have they learned her weaknesses yet?" asked Clarice.

He sighed and sat down on the couch. "Well, obviously she needs her wand, without it, she's not as powerful. Also, Mark. She spoils the crap out of him. He's her other weakness."

"Mark?" spat Kala. "That jerk is her son for real? That means..."

"He's our cousin."

Kala closed her eyes and groaned. "Thank *God* I never kissed him."

"That would have been disturbing," I said. "He knows we're cousins, too, I'm sure."

Clarice nodded. "Oh, yes I'm sure he does."

Rebecca walked into the room and sighed. "She wants to speak with you girls, just be careful not to touch her. The spell that's been cast upon her is like a poison. If you touch her, you'll be vulnerable to the curse as well."

"We can't touch her at all?" I asked.

"No. I'm sorry," replied Rebecca.

My sister and I looked at each other sadly.

"Let's go," I said, grabbing her hand.

"Follow me," said Rebecca, leading us down a long hallway.

We entered a beautiful, dimly-lit room on the other side of the house where our mother was now tucked inside of a luxurious king-sized bed.

"Come closer, just don't touch me," she murmured.

I stood over her and marveled at how fragile she looked. Not only was her face pale, but she looked almost gaunt, nothing like the healthy woman who'd fed me breakfast this morning. "I'm sorry," I whispered, with tears in my eyes.

"You have nothing to be sorry about," she sighed. "It's my fault. I should have told you a long time ago. I just didn't want you to get hurt."

"We understand," I said.

"What did you do to yourself?" asked mom.

I smiled sheepishly. "A potion, to lose weight."

"Oh, Kendra..."

"But mom, you wanted me to lose weight."

She shook her head. "I wanted you to be healthy. Potions are dangerous and not worth the risk. Please, don't ever do something like that again."

I nodded.

"Are you really going to die?" asked Kala. "Is it true?"

She swallowed. "Girls, I won't die and do you know why? Because you're going to destroy her."

I stared at her in shock. "Us? How can we do anything against *her*? She's a powerful sorceress."

Mom smiled. "She is not the only one. You two, together, can stop her."

"But we don't know the first thing about being a witch," argued Kala. "We know nothing of casting spells or witchcraft. I mean, all of this stuff was thrown on me fifteen minutes ago, although Kendra seems to have known about it much longer."

I frowned. "Hey, I just found out about it today, too. Cut me some slack."

She sighed. "Well, whatever. The point is we don't know how to be witches so there has to be another way."

Mom closed her eyes for a minute.

"Are you okay?" I asked.

She nodded and then reopened her eyes, which looked very tired. "Yes, just very weak from this... curse."

"I'm sorry for upsetting you, mom," whispered Kala.

She shook her head. "Oh, God, don't be. Now, I have something important to tell you. Listen to me carefully – in the attic there is an old trunk with all of my... secrets." She paused to catch her breath. "To unlock it, you only need to say, 'Michael, I love you', and then... it will open."

Michael was our father's name.

She went on. "I have a spell book in the trunk. In this book is a very powerful spell called 'Removal.' If you can get to that book and use the spell while you're standing before her, Vivian will disappear and... never bother any one of us again. She will be gone and the spell she's cast on me will also be removed. But, this is important, you *have* to say it and believe, without a doubt, that it will work."

Her eyes closed again and it looked like she'd stopped breathing.

"Mom?" I choked in horror.

"I'm... okay," she answered in a breathless whisper. She opened her haunted blue eyes up again and smiled weakly. "I'm still here."

"How much time do we have?" I asked, wishing I could do something for her right now.

She licked her lips, which were dry and cracked, as if something was sucking every ounce of life out of her. "You have twenty-four hours. Around four... tomorrow evening. But, I believe in you girls. You have it in you to defeat her, especially together. As a team. "

Kala looked at me. "Defeat her?"

I pursed my lips and nodded. "We have no choice. We have to try."

"Now, regardless of whether or not I make it, she must be stopped at all costs. If not, everyone will suffer. Her heart is as cold and black as death..." she whispered before her eyes rolled into the back of her head and she passed out.

Chapter Twenty-Four

Clarice stayed with our mother while the rest of us quickly teleported to "Secrets."

"So, what happens after we find this spell book? How are we supposed to get close enough to Vivian to perform it without her killing us first?" I asked, brushing the dust from my knees. I'd teleported with Tyler again, who obviously needed to work on his traveling skills, because we'd landed in a pile of discarded rags in the stockroom.

Rebecca raised her wand. "I'm going to keep her busy while you two recite the spell."

Tyler's face darkened. "Just be careful, mom."

She pulled her hair back and tied it into a ponytail. "Listen, I've had to deal with Vivian before. I can handle myself."

He sighed. "Yes, but Clarice told me that Vivian is already gaining power now that Adrianne is losing her own strength."

Kala and I looked at each other. We'd already lost our father, and the thought of losing our mom was too horrible to even imagine.

"We're going to park up the block and I'll keep an eye out for trouble while you guys sneak back to the house. I don't think Vivian will be hanging around, but you never know."

"Okay, let's get this over with before one of us chickens out," I said, noticing how tense Kala was.

Her eyes narrowed. "You're not talking about me, are you?"

"You do look pretty tense," said Tyler.

"Wouldn't you look tense, too," she snapped, "if your mother was dying, and you'd already lost your dad?"

Seeing the stricken look on Tyler's face, I winced.

"Believe it or not, I get it," he said, in an even tone.

"No, I don't think you really do," she mumbled, staring out the window.

"Kala," I said, "Tyler gets it more than *anyone*. Vivian already murdered his father."

She stared at him in horror. "Oh, my God. I'm so sorry. I didn't..."

"It's fine," he interrupted. "Let's just go and find her before she can hurt anyone else."

We all piled into Clarice's Buick, which was parked behind the store.

"Wouldn't it be easier just to teleport?" asked Kala.

"No, she'll sense it," said Tyler.

"Why didn't she show up at 'Secrets' then?" she asked.

"Because the shop is protected by one of my spells. Your house was, too, until Mark found out who you *really* were. Your mother told me that the house was only protected from Vivian, but not from Mark, because she wasn't aware of him."

"So, Mark can perform magic, too?" asked Kala.

Rebecca nodded. "Yes, he's a warlock, and now that he is honing his powers, he's potentially a very dangerous enemy."

"Jeez," I said, turning towards Kala. "And you thought he was cute."

"He must have put a spell on me," she muttered.

It was almost eight o'clock by the time we reached our neighborhood.

"I'm going first," said Tyler, as Kala and I followed him out of the car. "I'll send you a signal if I see any danger."

"Maybe we should go through the back alley," whispered Kala. "It's less conspicuous."

"I don't know about that," I said. "Tyler and I were attacked in the alley earlier. If she's around, it won't matter which way we go, she'll figure it out."

"Just keep your eyes on the trees," said Tyler.

"Why?" asked Kala.

"Vivian uses birds to spy on people," I answered. "Believe me, it's pretty freaky."

Tyler jogged down the street ahead of us and we crept through the darkness, both of us nervous and scared beyond belief.

"Is it just me, or do you feel like someone is watching us?" whispered Kala.

The hair on the back of my neck was standing straight up. "Oh, yeah. In fact, I feel like someone's going to jump out of the bushes at any moment."

She pointed. "Look, Tyler's already made it to the door," said Rebecca.

He turned to us and waved his arm, motioning us forward. We picked up our pace and quickly joined him on the porch.

"Door's open," he whispered. He pushed the door open slowly and we all stepped inside.

My eyes darted around the dark living room, the one I'd always felt so safe in. Even from where I was standing, the entire house seemed so quiet and normal, but the truth was, I was so frightened, I felt like throwing up. Every little sound freaked me out, from the furnace clicking on, to the tick-tock of our old grandfather clock.

"She said the trunk was in the attic," I whispered.

"I'm going to cast a protection spell on your house while you're in the attic," said Rebecca, appearing out of the nowhere.

"Oh, my God, don't do that," I whispered loudly. "You scared the crap out of me!"

"Sorry." She raised her wand in the air. "Something told me it wouldn't be wise to leave you children unattended. Now, this spell might not work, especially if Vivian has already casted a 'Spell Blocker', but it's definitely worth a try."

She then raised her wand and began to chant under her breath. Seconds later, a blast of light shot out of her wand and lit the corners of the house up.

"Crap," she said, as the light quickly died. "I don't think it worked. We need to find that book as quickly as possible."

"Okay, I'm going outside to watch the house and see if I can contact Trixie," said Tyler, moving down the hallway and towards the back door.

"Let's go," said Rebecca, walking towards the stairs.

"What's going on between you two?" whispered Kala as we followed Rebecca.

I looked at her. "I'm not sure yet."

"He's cute."

I smiled. "Yes, very."

"Is this your mom's room?" asked Rebecca, stepping inside.

"Yes," I answered. "The attic entrance is in her walk-in closet."

Rebecca stepped over to the closet and opened the door. I noticed that the smell of my mother's perfume still lingered in the air, and it was somewhat comforting.

"Have you ever been in the attic?" asked Rebecca, waving her wand up towards the entrance on the ceiling. It opened and a long white ladder materialized out of thin air.

"Uh, no, I don't think Kala and I have ever been up there. We were always afraid there'd be mice or bats hiding inside."

"Well, there very well could be," said Rebecca, climbing the ladder. "But right now, we should be more frightened of Vivian."

I couldn't agree more.

I followed her up the ladder with Kala close behind. When I stuck my head inside of the opening, I couldn't see much of anything in the darkness.

"Rebecca?" I whispered.

"Hold on." She raised her wand. "Light and Sparkle."

The next thing I knew, the attic began to light up and there was a whirlwind of movement all around. Moments later, there was a blast of light so bright, I had to cover my eyes. When it finally dimmed, I reopened my eyes and found the entire attic clean and organized.

"Nice. I wish I could do that," I smiled, standing up.

"You'll be able to soon enough," promised Rebecca, as Kala pulled herself inside.

"Look," I pointed towards the south corner of the attic, "that must be the trunk. I've never seen it before."

"Yes, indeed," said Rebecca as we moved towards it.

It was an old brown Victorian trunk with leather strap enclosures. I looked at Kala. "Um, remember, we have to say the words to open it."

"Oh, okay. Michael, I love you?" said Kala.

The trunk didn't even move.

"You have to say it with more feeling. Magic won't work if you aren't completely convinced that it will," reminded Rebecca.

I closed my eyes, took a deep breath, and said, "Michael, I love you."

"It's working!" cried Kala.

I opened my eyes and watched as the trunk's lid sparkled brightly and then popped open.

Kala squealed with delight. "You did it! I guess you're a true believer."

"After today, how could I not be?" I said, bending down to look inside.

There were several items in the trunk, including a wand, a broken broom, a few pieces of jewelry, and crystals. Right now, however, all of our attention was on the thick spell book at the bottom.

I picked up the old, leather-covered book and opened it up carefully.

"Be careful," whispered Rebecca.

I nodded. The pages were old and worn, obviously hundreds of years old.

"Have you ever seen this before?" I asked her.

She bent down on one knee. "No, but I believe it was your grandmother's. She was a very powerful witch."

"I saw a picture of her once, but mom never really said much about her. She was very secretive about a lot of things, now that I think about it."

"Well, it makes sense now, doesn't it?" muttered Kala. "Mom's a witch with many secrets."

"Something's amiss," said Rebecca, standing up quickly. Her brows furrowed. "I think Tyler's in danger. I'll be right back." She then raised her wand and disappeared.

"Let's bring the book downstairs," I said. "We'll need to find that spell and figure out how we're going to locate Vivian, too."

A sudden bright flash of light blinded both of us. I winced and covered my eyes.

"Find me?" chuckled Vivian. "I don't think that's going to be a problem."

My eyes snapped open and I stared in horror again at the woman who looked so much like our mother. She pointed her wand at us, but then suddenly appeared to have changed her mind. She smiled wickedly. "No... I think I'd rather have you around, so you can fully appreciate my powers, especially when your mother shrivels up and dies."

"Why do you hate her so much?" I hollered, horrified that she could be so heartless. "You're sisters! How can you be so cruel as to want her dead?"

Vivian's blue eyes narrowed. "Why? I suppose you wouldn't know. Your mother had many secrets and she probably wouldn't have shared this kind of information with you. She wouldn't want anyone to know what kind of a person she really was."

"We didn't even know she was a witch," muttered Kala.

"But we know she was a good person, one with a heart of gold," I said, raising my chin. Nobody was going to tell me otherwise.

Vivian snorted. "A heart of gold? No, she's a deceitful, lying, little fool who should have never tried to cross me."

I thought about this woman before me who'd killed Tyler's father and now wanted to destroy our family. I glared at her. "How did she cross *you*?"

"Your *loving* mother," she sneered, "took something that meant the world to me. She took it without regret and didn't care what it would do to me. She was the one who forgot that *we* were sisters."

"What did she take?" whispered Kala.

Vivian was suddenly distracted by the book in my arms. She pointed. "What's that?"

"Um, nothing," I replied, backing away.

"Give that to me, foolish girl," she hollered. "I know exactly what that book is and it was *my* mother's. It doesn't belong to you!"

I glared at her. "Obviously it doesn't belong to you, either. It's my mother's now."

Vivian raised her wand and the book vanished out of my hands and appeared in hers. She smiled in satisfaction. "I always wondered what happened to this old thing."

"Please," I begged her. "Take your hex off of our mother and keep the book. You really can't hate her that much?"

The look she gave me chilled me to the bone. "Oh, but I do."

"Tell us then why, at the very least," begged Kala.

She smiled bitterly. "Adrianne took something that could never be replaced. The man I loved with all of my heart. *Michael.*"

"Our father?" I gasped.

Her eyes filled with hate. "Yes, your father. I had Michael first but she stole him from me. And now," she smiled coldly, "I'm stealing her life away from her and I want everyone to suffer the way I have all of these years!"

"Mark?" I whispered in horror. "Mark is our brother?"

She smirked. "He's your *half*-brother, but only in blood." She smiled and lowered her voice. "He hates you both as much as I hate Adrianne."

Before I could respond, she clutched the spell book against her chest and disappeared with the only means we had to save our mother.

Chapter Twenty-Five

"What are we going to do?" cried Kala.

"I don't know," I whispered, horrified. "She has the book, obviously. I just don't know."

She grabbed my arm. "Let's go find Rebecca."

"Okay," I said, bending down into the trunk again. "Let's take mom's wand with us. It might be of some help."

"Good idea…oh, my God, what's happening?" gasped Kala, as the wand began to radiate in my hand.

"I don't know, but my fingers feel funny," I said, staring at my hand, which was beginning to glow and tingle.

"Maybe you should put that wand down."

"No," replied woman's voice.

It was coming from the wand!
Kala and I stared at each other in shock.
"Don't be afraid, dear," said the wand. "It's just part of the bonding process."
"Bonding process?" I squeaked.
"Yes," answered the wand, sounding amused. "I have to make sure we are compatible."
"Uh, what would happen if we weren't?"
"If you tried casting a spell and we weren't compatible, one of us would more than likely... perish."
"What?" I gasped, wanting to get rid of it.
"Don't let go of me, dear! You've passed the test and we are indeed compatible."
I breathed a sigh of relief as my hand stopped glowing and the tingling receded. "Wow, you frightened me there for a minute."
"Are all wands like you?" asked Kala.
"No. It just so happens that I was manifested in 1956 by Isadora Jenkins, a very powerful sorceress."
"Was she a good witch or a bad witch?" I asked.
"She didn't consider herself evil, but she did indeed practice the art of Black magic. Her

sister, Fedora, on the other hand, practiced only White, and I was created as a gift for her."

"Oh... so, you are a supposed to be used for White magic only?" I asked.

"Yes."

"If I dabbled in Black magic, we wouldn't be compatible, then?"

The wand hesitated and then spoke again. "It's a bit more complicated than that. I am only compatible with those who would not use magic specifically for their own personal gain. Some witches who practice White magic are still... not so pure of heart."

"Oh."

Kala smiled. "That must mean you're pure of heart."

"I didn't feel so pure yesterday when I was getting teased at school," I said. "If I would have had a wand and a chance to get rid of Mark or Hailey Bates, I wouldn't have thought twice about it."

"May I say something?" asked the wand.

"Uh, certainly," I said.

"Don't confuse your temporary emotions, like humiliation or sadness, with hate, greed, or malevolence. Even those pure of heart fall victim to the emotions caused by others.

Obviously, you are not capable of intentionally hurting others for personal gain. If you were, we wouldn't be having this conversation right now."

I didn't miss the meaning behind those words. If I was more like my aunt, I'd be dead.

"That's it!" I cried. "We have to find Rebecca!"

"What?" asked Kala.

"I know how to stop her," I said, my heart pounding in my chest as I raced out of the attic and flew downstairs.

"Seriously?" asked Kala, following me.

"Yes, I just hope it works. Rebecca!"

Just then, Rebecca materialized, her face stricken with grief.

"What... what's happened? Where's Tyler?" I asked, afraid of her answer.

"I don't know. I can't find him anywhere," she answered, tears in her eyes. "I think Vivian might have done something to him."

My stomach clenched.

Not Tyler, too!

"Vivian was just here," said Kala. "She has the spell book."

"We have to find her," said Rebecca. "Before she hurts Tyler and your mother…" She closed her eyes. "Before things get worse."

"Do you know where she'd be?" I asked.

She waved her wand and her purse appeared, floating next to her waist. "I have something that might lead us to her," she said, opening it up.

"What, a magical crystal ball?" asked Kala, looking hopeful.

She shook her head and pulled out a book. "No," she said, showing us the cover. "Your school's address book."

I snorted. "What?"

"When I registered Tyler for school during the summer, they gave me one."

Kala's eyes widened. "Do you really seriously think Vivian would list theirs when she registered Mark last year?"

"That's what I'm hoping," she said, looking through the pages. "It's a longshot, but I don't know what else to do."

"I know how to stop Vivian," I said.

Rebecca looked at me in surprise. "What do you mean? How?"

I held up my mother's wand. "Do you know about this wand?"

"I know it's your mom's," she said. "And that it's a very dangerous wand, one that you don't want to mess around with."

"Well, Kendra has bonded with the wand," blurted my sister. "Or it bonded with her, whatever the case may be."

"You have to be very careful with that thing," warned Rebecca. "Your mother told me years ago that she didn't even feel comfortable handling it. That's why she used a different one most of the time."

Kala's eyes widened. "Why? She was pure of heart, obviously."

"So, you know about that?" smiled Rebecca.

"The wand told us," I said.

She stared at the wand in amusement. "Ah… interesting. Your mother was never able to make it talk."

"Another finicky wand?" I asked, thinking of Clarice's.

She nodded. "I guess. Anyway, what did it say to you?"

I relayed my conversation with the wand and Rebecca's eyes lit up. "I'm not even sure if Adrianne was aware of how dangerous the wand could be to a malevolent witch. You know, this might just work."

"What?" asked Kala.

I turned to my sister, who obviously hadn't gotten it yet. "If we can get Vivian to use the wand, it just might destroy her."

Chapter Twenty-Six

"*Might* destroy her," said Rebecca. "She's already so powerful that the chances are pretty slim."

"Well, I say we go for it anyway," I said. "I mean, she has the spell book and you've pretty much stated that you can't stop her yourself. Kala and I are new to all of this and don't know the first thing about witchcraft. What other choice do we have?"

"Right now, none," agreed Rebecca.

"Did you hear that?" whispered Kala. "I think someone's outside."

"Don't worry, I think I know who this is," said Rebecca as she walked over to the front door opened it. Standing on the other side was Trixie and a guy whose features were similar.

Both of them had a soft glow about them that could only be described as... mystical.

"Trixie and Bailey," beamed Rebecca, stepping back. "Come in, please."

"We've come to help," said Trixie, who looked just as breathtaking and ethereal as earlier.

Rebecca's eyes lit up. "Do you know where Vivian has taken Tyler? Did you see anything?"

"I did," replied Bailey. He was tall, with broad shoulders and longish blond hair. "I followed them. Vivian cast a spell on Tyler and he was knocked unconscious. I believe he's still alive, though."

Rebecca put her hand on her chest and sighed in relief. "Oh, thank God, I was so worried."

"We'll find them," he said, placing his hand on her shoulder. "Don't worry, Rebecca."

"With Vivian, it's hard not to," she said.

He nodded and turned toward us. "You must be Adrianne's daughters?"

"Oh, God, where are my manners? I forgot to introduce you," said Trixie, raising her hand. "This is my brother, Bailey."

"Hi," I said shyly. I had to admit, he *was* gorgeous, with his silvery blue eyes and perfectly sculpted features, but truthfully, all I could think about was Tyler and my mother. "I'm Kendra."

We shook hands and then he turned to Kala whose own eyes were glazed over with adoration.

"You are clearly Kendra's sister," he said, smiling in amusement. Obviously, being fawned over was nothing new to him.

"Yes, I'm Kala," she answered, her cheeks turning pink. "So... um, are you a witch or some kind of warlock?"

"No. I'm a Shape-shifter," he answered, puffing his chest out a little.

"Oh, how... wonderful," she gushed, fluttering her eyelashes. "That must be so exciting."

He crossed his arms under his chest and nodded. "Well, yes, it certainly has its moments."

I bit my lip to keep from laughing.

"We don't have much time," interrupted Rebecca. "We need to find Tyler and stop the curse. Lead the way, Bailey."

He dropped his arms. "We'll need to teleport. They're in New York."

I raised my eyebrows. "New York?"

"Well, to tell you the truth... it makes perfect sense," said Rebecca. "With her interest in the theater and her music. I guess I should have figured that out before."

"Don't be so hard on yourself, Rebecca. She covers her tracks well," said Trixie. "It wasn't easy to follow either of them. It took Bailey a while before he actually found her real home in New York."

"So, they don't even live in Bayport?" I asked.

"They don't have to," said Bailey. "Vivan and Mark can teleport anywhere in the world."

I rubbed the bridge of my nose, feeling so vulnerable. How in the world was I going to help stop someone as powerful as Vivian? And right now our mother was dying and poor Tyler was at her mercy. My stomach tightened into a knot. "What do you think she wants with Tyler?"

Rebecca's eyes darkened. "Revenge, for what his father did. I have a feeling she'll torture him if we don't get moving. Bailey?"

"Let's move," he said. "Join hands and we'll teleport together."

"You know how to teleport?" asked Kala, reaching quickly for his hand.

He nodded. "There are many things us Shape-shifters have learned throughout the years."

"It also helps to have a mother and an aunt who are witches," smirked Rebecca. "Right, nephew?"

He grinned.

I joined hands with Trixie and Rebecca.

"Now, she lives in Long Beach, right near the ocean. There's a small wooded area behind her home and I'm going to aim for that," said Bailey.

"Let's go," said Rebecca.

I closed my eyes, and within seconds, felt myself being sucked into the vortex. This time I kept my eyes closed and pictured Tyler's face, praying we'd find him alive.

Chapter Twenty-Seven

"Get down," whispered Bailey when we landed in the darkness next to a swimming pool behind a white colonial mansion.

"I think we missed the woods but found the party," I said, staring at the impressive house in surprise. It was almost midnight, the place was lit up like a Christmas tree, and music flowed from somewhere inside.

"Definitely looks like a party," whispered Trixie, as dozens of shadows moved behind the curtained windows of the house. "This could be very bad."

"Or it might just make it easier for us to sneak inside," said Bailey.

"Who has a swimming pool when your house faces the ocean?" whispered Kala, as we crouched down and moved towards a light blue cabana for cover.

"Vivian," answered Rebecca. "The woman has an insatiable appetite for luxury when she isn't trying to destroy those she hates."

"It's amazing how totally different two twin sisters could be," said Kala. "Mom's not a spender and would never treat herself to anything. She won't even spend the money to get her hair cut."

"But it always looks good," I winked. "I think we now know why."

"Oh..." smiled Kala, "that makes sense."

"Okay, so here's the plan," interrupted Bailey. "Trixie and I will slip inside and look around."

"I don't know if it's going to be that easy. Vivian is probably having some kind of celebration," said Rebecca with a grim smile, "and I'm sure her guests aren't the kind you'd want to mess around with. They're probably part of her coven."

"Oh crap," I said, biting my lower lip. Dealing with Vivian was bad enough, but an entire coven of witches? It was too scary to imagine but too real to ignore. As far as I was concerned, things weren't looking very good for the White-witch team.

"Don't worry, Kendra," said Bailey, with a reassuring smile. "Danger isn't new to our world."

Could he also read minds?

He took a step back and seconds later, appeared before us as a sleek, white cat.

"Oh!" gasped Kala, her eyes round.

"Splendid idea," smiled Trixie. Then, in the blink of an eye, she changed into the form of a small gray mouse.

"Be careful," whispered Rebecca, as they took off towards the house, both on four legs.

"What should we do now?" I whispered, shivering. The wind was cool and I was kicking myself for not wearing any kind of jacket.

She rubbed her forehead. "We'll wait a bit for them to report back. If it takes too long, however, I'm going to try and find a way to get inside of the house."

"You said that Vivian could sense if we were close or if someone was using magic. How come she doesn't know we're here right now?" I asked. "Especially after teleporting?"

"Fortunately for us, she lives by the ocean, which sometimes blocks a witch's radar. If she knew we were here, I'm sure we wouldn't be having this conversation right now."

"Speaking of magic, can't you just use yours now to get us inside?" asked Kala.

"Unfortunately, no. She has a spell around her house, blocking any unwanted... guests," she said, closing her eyes. She raised her hands in the air and exhaled, slowly. "Try and see if you can feel it, too."

I closed my eyes and raised my hands. "Uh, sorry, I'm not feeling anything."

"I do," whispered Kala.

I turned to her in surprise. "What does it feel like?"

Her forehead wrinkled in concentration. "Um, it just kind of makes my skin tingle. Almost feels like pin-prickles, I guess."

"Yes," said Rebecca. "Very good."

"Why can't I feel it?" I asked, closing my eyes to try again.

"Because of me," stated my new wand, apparently in the chatting mood again.

I opened my eyes and stared at it in surprise. "You?"

"Yes. That menial spell of hers isn't strong enough to keep you out, as long as you have *me* in your possession," said the wand, in a smug tone.

"Awesome," I grinned.

"Just thought I'd put my two cents in. Now, carry on," said the wand.

"Wands aren't much for small talk, are they?" I asked after a few minutes of silence.

"No" replied Rebecca. "Some never even speak at all; which can sometimes be a good thing."

"I heard that, madam," snapped the wand. "Not amusing."

"I didn't mean you, personally. What is your name, by the way?" she asked the wand.

The wand didn't answer.

"See, they can be very stubborn," whispered Rebecca.

"I'm not daft," snapped the wand. "My name is Chloe. Now, if you'd like my advice, I would stop wasting precious time and send us into that house."

Surprisingly, I agreed. "I'm with Chloe. Something tells me that Tyler's time is running out, as well as our mother's."

Rebecca paled. "Okay, um...I just hate to send you in there alone..."

"She has me," said Chloe. "Now, prepare for our ascent, child."

I raised my eyebrows. "What?"

The next thing I knew, the wand began to glow and I soon found myself in a dark library.

"Stay still," whispered Chloe.

Before I could ask her why, a dog began to growl.

I whipped my head around towards the sound and found myself staring into the eyes of a large Doberman Pincher.

Chapter Twenty-Eight

"Uh, nice puppy?" I squeaked.

The dog growled louder and then began baring its teeth.

"Chloe, a little help?"

"Casting spells is your department, dear. I'm your instrument, not your instructor."

I raised the wand. "Uh...Go away?"

Nothing happened.

"Chloe?"

"Look, I can't do this for you, and in order for the spell to work, you need to actually have faith that it will. Try harder, witch."

Witch?

I pursed my lips. *That's right – I really was a witch, wasn't I?*

I took a deep breath, aimed the wand, and this time, put every ounce of faith in my command. "Depart!"

The dog turned around and bolted out of the room.

"Nice," I smiled, nodding in approval.

"Quickly, we must locate the boy and the Shape-shifters."

Crap.

"Are they *all* in trouble?"

"Yes," said the wand. "I believe so. I sense a growing frenzy down below."

"Shouldn't we tell Rebecca? So she can help?"

"There's no time. Prepare yourself."

Before I could protest, she transported me into a dark hallway in another part of the house, where I could hear several voices emulating from a nearby room.

"I say we keep *him* and kill the girl," snarled a woman with a deep, husky voice. "I'm sure we could find many uses for him."

"Behave, Beldora!" chuckled another woman. "He's much too young for you, anyway."

"I'm only one-hundred and seven… besides, he's a Shape-shifter – he's probably a century older than me!"

"Calm down, ladies," interrupted Vivian. "You can do whatever you'd like with these two.

My concern is that they're not here alone. We need to search the premises and destroy anyone not welcome. Now, we should go quickly."

Crap.

A doorway down the hallway flew open and I quickly pointed the wand at myself and whispered. "Hide, Invisible, Conceal."

The wand lit up and then disappeared, along with my arm, and hopefully – the rest of me.

The first two women who stepped out of the doorway stopped abruptly. Both wore black gothic-styled robes.

"Did you hear something?" asked the taller one with long, blonde hair and red-painted lips.

The other woman had dark hair pulled into a bun and piercing eyes that seemed to stare right through me from down the hallway. "I'm not sure."

"Quit dawdling," commanded Vivian, stepping around them. Her robe was made of red velvet, and obviously much more luxurious than the others. "We need to move quickly."

"Yes, Vivian," replied both women.

I watched in horror as ten other women, also dressed in black robes, stepped out of the room and began following Vivian, who was heading in my direction. All of the blood rushed to my ears.

Crap...crap...crap...

As they grew closer, I held my breath and pushed myself back against the wall, praying that they wouldn't somehow sense me there.

"What about Tyler?" asked the blonde with the ruby-red lips. "Have you made a decision yet?"

A cruel smile spread across Vivian's face as she passed me by. "I'm going to make sure his mother gets to watch him take his last breath, but not before I make them both suffer miserably."

Chapter Twenty-Nine

As soon as the witches were gone, I rushed down the hallway and entered what appeared to be some kind of large gathering room. Three blue sofas along with six gold-colored chairs were arranged in a circle, and lying on the floor in the center, were Trixie and Bailey in their human forms.

"Oh, my God, what happened?" I asked, moving towards them.

"Spell," replied Bailey in a hoarse voice.

Both of their faces were twisted in pain, and although I couldn't see any restraints, it was obvious that they were somehow being subdued.

I raised the wand and started spouting off commands. "Release curse! Immunity! Remove Bonds!"

"You're wasting your time," sighed Chloe. "I can't remove this curse."

"Chloe? How can I help?" I whispered loudly. "They're in horrible pain. How can we stop it?"

"Kill Vivian," replied a familiar voice.

I turned around and found him hanging, in what appeared to be, some kind of human birdcage.

"Oh, thank God, Tyler!" I cried, rushing towards him. Thankfully, he appeared to be in good health and not suffering, like the Shape-shifters.

"Kendra? Is it really you? Where in the heck are you?" he asked, staring right past me.

"I'm invisible." I touched his fingers through the cage. "Are you all right?"

He smiled grimly. "Oh, I'm peachy. These witches really know how to throw a shindig."

I smiled. "I know you can't see me, but... I'm *so* happy to see you." My lips began to tremble. "I thought she might have…"

His squeezed my fingers. "Hey, it's okay. I haven't been hurt, just made a little uncomfortable in this stupid cage. Nothing like Bailey and Trixie." His face darkened. "She's placed some kind of spell, rendering them helpless and obviously in a lot of pain."

Just then, Mark stepped through the doorway. "Talking to yourself, vampire?" he asked with a smirk.

Tyler released my fingers and moved away. "Look who's talking, *witch*."

Mark scowled. "I'm a *warlock,* imbecile, and it would be wise to show me some respect if you'd like to live another hour."

Tyler's face grew serious and he stared at him with intensity.

Mark snorted. "Don't even try it, Enchanter, mother has placed a spell on me, to protect me from your lame antics."

Tyler sneered. "Need mother to protect you, huh?"

"Obviously, you do as well – otherwise you wouldn't be here in the first place."

"Why don't you let me out of this cage and we'll settle this like two guys instead of our mothers'... pets? Or don't you believe you're man enough?"

Mark's eyes narrowed. "You couldn't put me down if I *let* you. You're a skinny little twerp who doesn't know when to shut his hole."

"Just what I thought, you're scared of me," chuckled Tyler, staring at his nails.

His face grew red and he clenched his fists at his side. "Screw you. I could take you with my hands tied behind my back."

"Is that right?"

"Hey, I know what you're doing, freak. You're just trying to trick me into letting you out."

"Even if you let me out, I'm surrounded by witches. That must make you feel safer, hiding behind the skirts of all of these women."

"Shut up, douchebag!"

Tyler folded his arms across his chest. "Obviously, you can't make me. Not by yourself."

Mark's eyes burned with hate. "That's it. You want to fight? Fine. I'm not afraid of you! Your powers are *dead* here, Enchanter!" he spat, pulling out a long, skinny wand from his back pocket. He aimed it at the cage. "You want to use bare knuckles? Well, I'm down with that. Release!"

The cage door opened and I held my breath.

Tyler crawled out and then stood up, facing Mark. "What are you waiting for?" he asked with a cocky grin.

Mark put his wand back into his pocket and before I could blink, launched himself at Tyler, knocking him backwards and onto the wood-paneled floor.

"You think I need magic to break you, smartass?" growled Mark, who was now on top of Tyler and pulling his fist back. "Think again!"

Before Mark could follow through with his punch, Tyler reached up, grabbed him by the neck, and shoved his aside with more strength than I would have thought he had. Then he moved behind Mark, slid his arm around his neck, and put him in a choke-hold. After a few seconds, Mark's eyes rolled into the back of his head and he went limp.

"Oh, my God," I gasped, still in shock. "Is he dead?"

"No, just unconscious for a bit. Here, take his wand," he said, holding it out to me.

I grabbed it. Fortunately, it didn't try bonding with me. "What now?"

"Cast a spell."

My eyes widened. "Can't you?"

He frowned. "No, remember they've put some kind of spell on me. My powers aren't working at the moment."

"But you can use a wand, can't you?"

He shook his head. "A wand will only work for a true witch."

"But you're half witch, aren't you?"

"Half warlock, but I've never been able to use a wand. They just don't seem to work for me."

"Oh." I held out my own wand and pointed it towards Mark. "Uh, disappear!?"

Nothing happened.

"Be gone!" I called out, shrilly.

Tyler rubbed the bridge of his nose. "You really don't know what you're doing, do you?"

"Obviously, no," I said, suddenly angry. "This is *all* new to me. I mean, I haven't had any training, none whatsoever. So guess what?" I raised my voice. "I'm freaken' winging it!"

"Sorry," he said, looking embarrassed and hurt.

I closed my eyes and sighed. "No, *I'm* sorry," I said. "You didn't deserve that."

Just then, Mark opened his eyes and reached for Tyler. I pointed my wand at him and hollered, "Depart, dark warlock!"

This time, he disappeared into thin air.

"Where'd he go?" I whispered.

Tyler stood up and brushed off his pants. "Does it really matter?"

"I guess not."

Bailey started moaning again. I turned around and stared at him, feeling so helpless. "Tyler, we have to help those two. I almost forgot."

"Try using Mark's wand," he said, moving towards Trixie, who now appeared to have passed out from whatever pain she was feeling. "Since he's Vivian's son, you might be able to somehow reverse the spell."

"Can you actually do that? Reverse someone else's spell?"

"I don't really know. But, it's worth a shot."

I stared at Mark's wand and bit the side of my lower lip. "His wand is probably used for Black magic, though, don't you think?"

He shrugged. "It doesn't matter. You should still be able to use it."

I was about to tell him about my wand and what a mistake it would be if anyone else tried using it when Vivian materialized next to Tyler. Fortunately, I was still invisible.

"How did you get out of the cage, and *where* in the world is Mark?" she snarled, her blue eyes blazing with fury.

"He let me out," smirked Tyler, "and then left to get us some tacos. If you're nice, I'll share some with you."

She scowled. "You think you're pretty funny, don't you? Well, something is definitely amiss, here… but," she smiled triumphantly. "I know how to correct it." She then snapped her fingers.

"Mother!" hollered Tyler, as Rebecca and Kala materialized with their captors, four of Vivian's witches.

"Tyler," she replied, her eyes filling with tears. "Thank goodness, you're okay."

"What happened to them?" gasped Kala, staring at Bailey and Trixie, who were now both, apparently, unconscious.

"The same thing that's going to happen to you if you don't tell me where your meddling sister is," snarled Vivian.

"I… I really don't know," said Kala, taking a step backwards.

Vivian moved closer and grabbed her by the jaw. She grinned evilly. "Do you think that just because we're family, I'd hesitate to kill you?"

Kala's eyes filled with tears. "No, I'd never make any assumptions about you. I swear."

Vivian stared at Kala for a few more seconds and then released her chin. "Good girl, now tell me where she is or I'll kill your friends, starting with... him," she said, pointing towards Tyler. She wrinkled her nose. "He's already giving me a headache."

"Don't you dare touch him," snapped Rebecca.

"Oh, and what are *you* going to do about it?" asked Vivian, moving towards her. She put her hands on her hips, and with a haughty look, snarled, "You pathetic little twit. You can't save him or anyone else in this room. You couldn't even save your husband," she smiled coldly, "could you?"

Tyler roared in rage and launched at Vivian, who immediately held out her hand and hollered, "Freeze!" stopping him before he could reach her.

"Tyler," choked Rebecca, breaking away from one of the witches and rushing to his side.

Unfortunately, he was frozen in place, his face turning a frosty white and his lips a deep blue.

"Oh, my God!" cried Kala, putting her hand over her lips.

I couldn't take it anymore. I aimed my wand at Vivian and cried, "Depart!"

She disappeared.

"It worked?" I laughed, not quite believing my eyes. "Seriously?"

The other four witches raised their own wands in retaliation, but I'd been prepared for that. I pointed Chloe at them and hollered, "Depart!" They too disappeared and I squealed in joy.

Rebecca shook her head. "No, it can't be that easy."

"Maybe it can," I said excitedly. "Now, I just have to figure out a way to become visible." I pointed the wand at myself and said, "Materialize."

Nothing happened.

"Try 'Appear'," said Rebecca, who was now crouched down next to Bailey and Trixie.

"Appear."

"Kendra," smiled Kala, rushing over and throwing her arms around me. "I was so worried about you."

"You should be more worried about yourself," cackled Vivian, materializing next to her.

"No!" gasped Kala.

Vivian turned to me and smiled coldly. "Did you think you could get rid of me that easily, child? You obviously don't know what you're doing."

I glared at her. "The one thing I do know is that you're an evil woman and obviously didn't deserve our father."

Her eyes narrowed. "That's enough from you."

I raised my wand and yelled "Depart" once more, but this time, nothing happened.

She patted her long, red hair and smiled. "You're such a novice."

Rebecca pulled out a wand from her jacket, pointed it towards Vivian, and cried, "Terminate."

Nothing happened.

"See, your powers are useless here. What interests me, however," said Vivian, moving towards me. "Is how *you* were able to cast a spell?"

My heart began to race as set my plan in motion. I took a step backwards. "I'm not going to tell you unless you release our mother from your curse, as well as the Shape-shifters."

She threw her head back and laughed. "Clearly, you must be joking!"

"No, I'm serious," I said, raising my wand again. "Be seated!" I cried.

"How?!" she raged, her butt now planted in one of the gold chairs.

"The wand," blurted my sister, obviously knowing where I was going with this. "It's better than yours."

"Nonsense," hissed Vivian, getting up from the chair. She raised her own wand. "My wand was created by the great Isadora. There is *nothing* more powerful than this wand, I assure you."

"Well, her wand was made by a powerful wizard," said Kala. "And we can assure you that there is nothing like it in all the world."

I held my breath, wondering if there really were wizards and if Vivian would actually fall for it.

Her eyes searched mine and I tried not to blink. "A wizard created it, you say? How do you girls know this?" asked Vivian.

"The wand told me," I said.

Her eyebrows shot up. "Your wand speaks?"

"Yes. All the time." I smiled. "It tells me…. secrets."

"Secrets?" She held out her hand and snapped her fingers. "Give it to me and… I'll let you leave here unscathed."

I smiled coldly. "The only way I'm giving you this wand is if you remove all of the curses, including my mother's."

She snorted. "Don't be ridiculous."

I shrugged. "You know, I think this wand is much too powerful for you anyway."

"Ignorant girl, *nothing* is too powerful for me."

I made no move to give her the wand.

She sighed. "Okay, fine… hand me the wand and I'll let you leave here with your friends."

I leaned forward. "Release our *mother* from your curse and I'll *give* you the wand."

She pointed her wand at Kala. "Enough of these games – say goodbye to your sister."

"No!" I shrieked, holding up my hand. "Wait!"

Vivian lowered her wand.

"Uh, take the curse off of the Shape-shifters and Tyler, and I'll give you the wand freely."

She stared at the wand in my hand and swore under her breath. "Okay, fine." Then she aimed her own wand at Bailey and Trixie. "Release!"

The Shape-shifters' faces both relaxed, as did their bodies. Seconds later, they were both on their feet, looking exhausted and confused, but no longer in pain.

"Are you okay?" I asked Trixie, as Bailey held her up. She was much paler than her brother, and obviously not quite as resilient.

She smiled weakly. "Nothing a few cups of coffee couldn't cure. Thank you, Kendra."

"Or a few dead witches," said Bailey, glaring at Vivian.

"Don't test me, shifter," snapped Vivian. "If you want to keep that gorgeous face of yours."

He frowned but didn't answer.

"What about Tyler?" I asked.

Sighing, Vivian aimed the wand towards him and bellowed, "Defrost!"

"Thank goodness," Rebecca cried, rushing to his side as he began to thaw. She threw her arms around him and began rubbing his pale cheeks, bringing color to his face.

"Mom," he mumbled. "Too tight."

"Sorry," she said, loosening her grip.

"You okay?" I asked him.

"Other than being as cold as her heart, I'm doing okay," he answered.

Vivian ignored his snide comment. "Now, give me the wand," she demanded.

I took a deep breath and held it out to her. "Take it, it's yours."

Chapter Thirty

Vivian stepped forward and took the wand from me. Within seconds, it began to glow in her hand. She smiled, triumphantly. "Ah... it's a bonding wand, just like mine."

Kala and I glanced at each other.

"Yes," breathed Vivian, her blue eyes gleaming with satisfaction. "The power inside of this wand is great; I can feel it coursing through my veins."

"How *does* that feel?" I asked, wondering if I'd made a horrible mistake. *Was it possible that the wand would add to her strength? Had I been misled?*

"It feels..." her eyes widened in surprise. "What...what's happening?"

I didn't say anything, just watched in wonder as her hand began to glow. Unlike mine, however, it was a bright, crimson color.

"No," she gasped, now trying to shake the wand out of her hand. "No!"

The red light started to spread, traveling up her arm, into her face, and from what I guessed, throughout the rest of her body.

"What have you done?!" she bellowed. "What's happening to me?"

I watched her face contort in pain and anguish as the wand's magic continued its assault and my feelings were muddled. As evil as she was, Vivian was still my mother's twin, and watching her go through so much agony was unsettling.

"Help me!" she screeched, falling to her knees. She reached up and began pulling at her long, red hair. "Please," she sobbed, "someone, stop this!"

Seeing her so helpless and frightened reminded me of my mother and my heart suddenly cried out for her. No matter how much pain she'd already caused everyone else, she was still part of my family and mom's twin sister. There was no way I could stand by and watch her suffer this way anymore.

There had to be another way.

My eyes welled up with tears and I took a step forward to try and help her, when Rebecca placed a hand on my shoulder. "Don't."

"But she's dying!" I cried.

"So is your mother," she reminded me. "Listen." She moved until she was blocking my view of Vivian. "There is no other way to save your mom. It's Vivian's fate or your mom's. If she survives, your mother *will* most certainly die, and eventually, Vivian will come for all of us."

I turned towards Kala, who, surprisingly, looked very calm. She caught me staring and smiled grimly. "It *has* to be this way. For mom's sake."

Letting out a ragged sigh, I nodded and wiped my tears.

Tyler moved closer to me and put an arm around my shoulders. "Hey," he whispered into my ear. "I think it's over."

Sighing, I stepped around Rebecca and looked down at Vivian, whose eyes were now closed. I watched as the red glow receded from her skin. From the stillness of her body, it was obvious there was no life left inside of her.

"Let's go check on mom," I said, wiping a few more stray tears. "Hopefully, this worked, and she's been set free from the curse."

Just then, three more witches materialized in the room.

"What have you done?" cried the blonde I'd seen in the hallway earlier. She rushed to Vivian's side and kneeled down. "Vivian?"

Rebecca raised her wand and whispered, "This is our cue to leave."

"You're not going anywhere," said the dark-haired witch with the bun, her wand raised threateningly.

"She's dead!" screeched the blonde witch, her eyes filled with rage. "Vivian's dead!"

"Who killed her?" asked the third witch, an older woman with grayish-black hair and a broad nose.

"None of us," I said, raising my chin. "It was the wand."

The older witch walked over to my wand, which now lay on the floor, and her face turned pale. "I know this wand. It used to be Adrianne's. I'm surprised Vivian didn't notice that."

The blonde reached for it.

"Don't touch it!" hollered the older witch, stepping back.

She pulled her hand away. "Why not, Semora?"

"It's dangerous, Bella," she said, her eyes wide. She pointed towards Vivian. "You see what it did to her."

Bella stood up and backed away from the wand. "So, it really was the wand that killed her?"

"I told you," I said. "Only those who aren't out for personal gain can handle the wand. Obviously, Vivian was only out for herself."

Semora turned towards me. "You two," she said, glancing at Kala as well, "are Adrianne's daughters, aren't you?"

"Yes," we both replied.

Her lips thinned and she nodded. "Very well. I, personally, never had anything against Adrianne. In fact, your aunt probably had what was coming to her."

"What?!" gasped Bella. "How can you say that? She was the head of our coven!"

Semora sighed. "Oh, come on. We were just talking about how unstable Vivian was getting."

"No," she snapped. "Vivian wasn't just our leader, she was my best friend." She looked at me and scowled. "Wand or not, I'm going to make sure all of you pay for her death. Come on, Beldora, let's go tell the others!"

Beldora nodded and then both witches disappeared.

"You'd better leave," said Semora. "They'll return with the others and you won't have a chance against that many wands." She then disappeared.

"Grab yours," said Rebecca, pointing towards Chloe.

I stared at the wand in fear. "Uh, what if..."

"What if what?"

"I wanted Vivian to die," I said, looking down in shame. "That means that my heart isn't pure anymore. I guess I'm just too frightened to touch the wand now."

"Did you really want to destroy Vivian, or did you just want your mother safe?" asked Rebecca.

I glanced over towards Vivian. "I guess I would have rather had nobody die, and my mother safe."

She touched my shoulder and smiled. "That's what I thought. You're still a good person, Kendra, and in my heart I know there's nothing to worry about. Now, grab the wand. You're going to need it."

I walked over to the wand and bent down. Still struggling with uncertainty and fear, I took a deep breath and picked it up.

"It's okay, child," said the wand as my hand began to glow a warm yellow. "Don't be frightened."

I closed my eyes and released a sigh of relief. "Thanks, Chloe."

"You're welcome."

Tyler walked over to me and grinned. "You do realize now that you're claiming this wand as yours, you're going to need proper training?"

"Actually, I'm not claiming it as mine," I said. "It's my mother's and I'm going to make sure that she gets it back."

"No, it's yours now."

I gasped and turned towards the sound of her voice. "Mom?"

She smiled and it seemed to light up the room. "Surprise," she said, opening up her arms.

"Mom!" gasped Kala, flinging herself at her.

My eyes filled with tears as I rushed over and joined them. "Thank God you're okay."

"I love you both, so much," she murmured, squeezing us tightly. She kissed the tops of each of our heads. "I... I'm so relieved you're both okay. I prayed she wouldn't hurt you."

"We're fine, but what about you? Are you really okay?" I asked, pulling away to look into her face.

She nodded. "Yes, honey. I'm much better. I'm not exactly sure what happened, but you removed the curse."

"It was the wand," said Kala as she mom released us. "Your old wand, actually. It's what killed Vivian."

"Of course. I can't believe I hadn't thought about Isadora's wand." She turned towards her sister's body and I watched as her lower lip began to tremble. She closed her eyes and then reopened them. "Believe it or not," she said, her eyes glossy with tears, "I really loved Vivian. As much hate as she had for me, I still loved her."

"But why did she hate you so much?" I asked. "And what happened between her and our father?"

Her face paled. "She told you?"

I nodded. "Yes, but –"

"Sorry to interrupt, but we have to leave," said Clarice, materializing next to mom. "Vivian's coven is coming, and they're not happy."

My mother grabbed both of our hands.

"Meet us at Secrets," said Rebecca. "You'll be safe there."

Chapter Thirty-One

After we arrived at the shop, Bailey and Trixie were given some kind of potion to help them recover fully, Tyler went in search of food, and my mother stepped in the back warehouse to talk with Rebecca and Clarice.

"He's so cute," whispered my sister, staring at Bailey as he stood up and stretched. "I wonder if he has a girlfriend?"

I chuckled. "Probably a ton."

She sighed. "Yeah, I'm sure you're right."

"Girls," motioned mom from the back of the shop. "It's time we had that talk."

"Do you think?" muttered Kala under her breath as we started towards the back of the store. "It would have saved us a lot of trouble if she would have given us this talk a month ago."

"She was just trying to protect us," I reminded her.

"Which almost got all of us killed."

"Hey, I know."

When we stepped into the backroom, I stopped dead in my tracks – it looked like an entirely different place.

"What happened?" I asked Rebecca, who was sitting next to a large fireplace, drinking a cup of coffee with Clarice.

She smiled sheepishly. "Oh, well now that we don't have to hide our magic, I spruced up the place."

"I'll say," I said, looking around. Instead of a storage warehouse, it looked more like some kind of lodge, with two large oversized brown leather sofas, two recliners, a bearskin rug and even a stocked bar – except this one appeared to be supplied with bottles of different potions instead of booze.

Mom motioned us towards one of the sofas. "Please, sit down."

Kala and I sat down and then looked at her expectantly. She'd changed into jeans and a green wool sweater, her hair now a vibrant red.

"So that's your normal hair color?" asked Kala.

She nodded. "Yes. I hope you don't mind that I've changed it back. It's nice not having to hide anymore from Vivian."

"It's just weird," I said. "You look so much like Vivian."

"On the outside we're identical, but on the inside, we were never similar," she replied, her face melancholy.

"It's okay, mom," I said. "You shouldn't have to hide anymore. Besides, you look beautiful as a redhead."

She smiled. "Thanks. Well, I suppose I should start. Don't mind Clarice or Rebecca," she said, sitting down across from us in the other sofa. "I want them here, in case you have a question that I might not be able to answer."

I licked my lips. "Okay."

"Now," she sighed and sat back against the seat cushion. "I'm sure you're both pretty angry with me for keeping all of this from you."

"A little," I said. "But, we kind of understand."

She nodded and smiled sadly. "I, uh, I have something else to tell you that..." her eyes filled with tears. "Something I never *wanted* to tell you, but I know that I must. You have the right to know."

I leaned forward. "What?"

She burst out crying.

"Oh, my God, are you okay, mom?" asked Kala, moving next to her on the sofa. She took her hand. "Maybe we should wait until you feel better?"

She shook her head and then snapped her fingers. A box of tissues appeared. "Oh, God," she sobbed. "I hope you're not going to hate me for this."

"What is it?" I whispered, my stomach clenching in fear. Something told me that whatever she had to tell us was going to be far more substantial than anything I'd heard in the last twenty-four hours.

She wiped her face with a tissue and let out a ragged sigh. "Okay, I'm just going to have to start from the beginning."

I went and sat down on the other side of her. She grabbed my hand.

She took a deep breath. "My father murdered my mother and my sister murdered him."

"What?" I gasped.

She smiled grimly. "Talk about a dysfunctional family, huh?"

"What happened?" I asked, still in shock.

"Well, as you're aware of now, Vivian and I come from a long line of witches. Powerful witches. Well," she sighed, "my father was a preacher and he had no clue of who he'd actually married. In fact, when he found out that my mother was practicing witchcraft, he went after her in a blind rage and ended up shooting her. In turn, Vivian killed him."

"Well, that's not entirely surprising," said Kala. "I'm sure she was upset knowing that he killed your mother and did it out of blind rage."

"Yes but the thing was, Vivian enjoyed it."

"After meeting her, that doesn't surprise me one bit," I said.

"Mom, you never really mentioned your parents, did they love each other?" asked Kala.

She paused. "I know that my mother loved my father and that's why she didn't reveal what she really was. In fact, she stopped practicing witchcraft for many years, until we moved back to Salem, where she'd lived as a young girl. You see, my father was transferred to Salem by his church, to help crucify women who were charged with performing witchcraft. How ironic, huh?"

"So, that's when she started practicing it herself again?" I asked.

She nodded. "Yes, she was horrified at what my father was trying to do and started attending the ceremonies in the middle of the night. Eventually, my mother told Vivian and me about our heritage and we wanted to learn more. In fact, it was supposed to be our induction into the coven on the night they were both killed."

"Did your mother practice Black magic or White magic?" I asked.

"She never really said, but I believe she practiced White."

"So, what happened after your parents were killed?" asked Kala.

She smiled and turned towards Rebecca, who was listening in. "I moved in with Rebecca and her mother. They basically saved my life by taking me in."

Rebecca smiled warmly. "My mother loved you as if you were part of the family."

"What about Vivian?" I asked. "What happened to her?"

She turned back to me and her face became grave. "Vivian left that night and I didn't see her for seven years. She just...

disappeared off the face of the Earth. But when she returned…"

"What?" I asked.

She looked down at her hands. "At first, Vivian seemed like her old self. She was bubbly, excited about life, and… in love."

"She was in love?" I asked, afraid of what she was going to say next.

She nodded and looked up at me. "Yes, she was in love with Michael, your father."

"Oh, my God," I sighed. "Did he love her?"

"He thought he did, but then things changed."

"What happened?" whispered Kala.

She closed her eyes and let out a ragged breath. "She became pregnant."

Chapter Thirty-Two

"What?" I gasped. "Was the baby his?"

She stared at both of us and then her lower lip began to tremble. "Yes. They both were. Twin girls."

The blood rushed to my ears. "No," I said, standing up. "I don't want to hear any more of this."

Tears rolled down her cheeks. "He had the babies and Michael stood by her side, he even proposed to her but..."

"What?" whispered Kala.

"She never wanted the babies. She'd actually planned on giving them up and telling Michael that they'd both died during childbirth, but he'd found out beforehand and talked her into keeping them."

"Us, you mean?" I said. "He talked her into keeping us."

She started sobbing. "Yes, honey, I'm sorry. You and Kala are Vivian's biological daughters, but... *I* raised you. *I* did. And I've loved you more than that woman could have ever loved you, I swear to God!"

Kala and I stared at each other in shock.

Rebecca walked up behind Adrianne and put a hand on her shoulder. "Honey, do you want me to finish the story?"

She shook her head and dabbed at her tears with a tissue. "No, I need to finish this myself."

"What happened?" I asked, my voice hoarse.

"Please, sit back down," she pleaded, patting the seat cushion beside her. "Please."

I sat back down and she took my hand.

"What happened next?" asked Kala, her eyes also filled with tears.

She took a deep breath. "Michael bought them a home and they were going to be married after the two of you were born. Well, the night she went into labor, Vivian disappeared."

"What?" I gasped.

"Yes. From what I'd found out later, she'd went to a midwife and paid her a large sum of money to keep you. When she returned to

Michael two days later, she claimed she'd lost the both of you in childbirth."

"Oh, my God," mumbled Kala. "She paid someone to keep us? Who does that?"

"Apparently our real biological-slash-psychotic mother," I said dryly.

"Anyway, Michael didn't believe it, especially because she was so happy. In fact, at first, he thought maybe she'd just had a nervous breakdown and would eventually pull out of it and share in the sorrow of losing their children – but it never happened. She never mourned your loss, and that's when he started drifting away from her."

"How did he find out that we were still alive?" I asked.

"I told him," she said. "After I used my magic to find you."

I squeezed her hand. "Thank you."

She smiled sadly. "Of course, baby."

Kala wiped the tears that were now sliding down her cheeks. "What did she say when he confronted her about us?"

She closed her eyes and rubbed her forehead. "She was angry – furious at me. She tried attacking me, claiming that I was trying to ruin her life. She swore revenge and Michael finally saw the kind of hatful rage that she possessed. He was not only scared for you, but for his own life as well."

"She tried hurting the both of you?" squeaked Kala. "As in, *kill*?"

She grabbed Kala's hand and nodded. "Tried, but she never succeeded. In fact, that was the very same night that Michael and I rescued the both of you. We left Salem for good and never looked back."

"Is that when you realized you loved each other?" I asked.

She shook her head. "No, honey. At that time we both loved you and were not romantically involved. Michael asked me to help him escape with you two girls that night, and I did, without question. Eventually, over time, we fell in love and decided that I'd raise you as my own. We eventually got married and you pretty much know the rest."

"How come you never had any of your own children?" asked Kala.

"What do you mean? I had you girls," she smiled. "You're all I've ever wanted. As far as I'm concerned, you *are* my children. I... hope you feel the same way."

Kala and I both snuggled up to her at the same moment, like we did when we were really young.

"You're our mother," I whispered, resting my head on her shoulder. "Nothing else matters."

She loved us and had risked her life to protect us. As far as I was concerned, she was not only our mother, but our guardian angel.

"Yes," said Kala. "We love you so much, mom. Don't ever doubt it."

"Thank you," she answered, her voice thick. "You don't know how much that means to me."

We sat there silently for a while and then Clarice cleared her throat. "I hate to interrupt, but it's getting really late and I'm sure everyone's exhausted. I think we need to decide what's going to happen next."

"What do you mean?" I asked, sitting up.

The older woman scratched her head. "Well, now that Vivian's coven knows where you live, it's not safe going back to your house. You're going to need a new place to live."

Mom nodded. "She's right."

"You could stay with us in Vail," said Rebecca.

"That might work," said Clarice. "For now."

"I couldn't burden you," replied mom. "You've already done so much for us."

"Oh, it's not a bother. You're my friend and I've missed you so much," replied Rebecca.

Clarice sighed. "Actually, you are going to need each other." She looked at Rebecca. "Frankly, you're in just as much danger as Adrianne, so right now you *should* stick together." She tapped her chin thoughtfully. "Speaking of which, I think it might be time to get in touch with some of the members of *my* old coven."

"That might be a good idea," replied mom, standing up. "We could use all the help we can get."

"I agree," said Rebecca. "We may have started a real war by killing Vivian and should be prepared for anything. Once they find Mark, which I'm quite certain they probably already have, he's going to want revenge, as will her coven."

Mark, I'd forgotten all about him.

"Oh, my God," gasped Kala. "I almost kissed my brother!"

"Half-brother," I reminded her.

"Who cares, it's still pretty gross," she answered with a grimace.

"What I don't understand is why she kept Mark, but didn't want us?" I said.

"I've been wondering that myself," said mom. "He's obviously around your age and she would have had to have gotten pregnant soon after you were born."

"Mark isn't her real son," stated Clarice. "I found this out tonight from Semora, although I'm surprised I hadn't known about it myself."

I stared at her in shock. "What?"

"Not only that, Mark is going to be a very powerful warlock, once he hones his skills. In fact, he's Isadora's son."

I gasped. "You're serious?"

She nodded. "Oh, Yes. Vivian knew that and after his real mother died, she decided to raise him as her own."

"How did she die?" asked Kala.

"Isadora was ultimately killed by *her* sister. She was cursed, actually." Her lips twisted into a secretive smile. "Care to guess who her sister was?"

"I have no clue," answered mom.

"Your mother, Lisbeth. She was Isadora's sister."

"What?! But, how can that be? Mother never mentioned anything about having a sister," said mom.

"She was hiding from Isadora the same way you were hiding from Vivian. From what I learned, they had a falling out and Lisbeth placed a curse on Isadora."

"What kind of curse?" I asked.

"Should Isadora ever try harming another person using her magic, she'd perish. Well, after Isadora gave birth to Mark, Vivian apparently showed up at her doorstep in a pickle and asked her to help destroy you, Adrianne. She wanted revenge for stealing Michael. Obviously, Isadora tried and it became her demise."

"Oh, my goodness," whispered mother. "How come you never told me any of this before, Clarice?"

"That's because my mother never told me anything about it. I only found out about you from my own mother's diary, ten years ago. She was obviously very frightened of her younger sisters."

"Clarice, your mother was Isadora and Lisbeth's older sister?" asked Kala. "I'm so confused."

Clarice nodded. "Yes, there was actually four sisters all together. My mother was the oldest, then Isadora, Lisbeth, and Margaritte, who was the youngest. Nobody knows what happened to Margaritte."

"So, um, did you get Chloe from your mother?" I asked Adrianne.

Her eyebrows shot up. "Who's Chloe?"

"The wand you've given me," I said.

Adrianne smiled. "That's right, Chloe talks to you. Our connection wasn't as strong as yours. No, I didn't get Chloe from my mother."

"I gave it to her," said Clarice. "I knew that she wouldn't have a chance against Vivian, without it. Chloe belonged to my mother."

"Did anyone grab Vivian's wand?" asked Kala.

"No," I said. "And it's probably a good thing because if it's a bonding wand, then it could destroy anyone not meant to use it."

"That is very true," said Clarice. "Unfortunately, I'm sure Mark will eventually retrieve it, making him even more powerful."

"I think we should get moving soon," said Rebecca. "Something tells me we don't have much time. That they might be coming for us pretty quickly. I'm sure Mark is aware of this shop."

Kala and I stood up.

"What about Bailey and Trixie?" asked Kala. "Are they coming with?"

"No," replied Clarice. "They're needed here in Bayport. They can keep an eye on things for us and communicate with the other witches in town."

"There are other witches in Bayport?" asked Kala.

"Adele," I said. "Megan's mom. She's a witch, isn't she?"

My mother nodded. "Yes. I haven't spoken to her in years, but she is."

"Can we trust her?" asked Kala.

"The truth is, it's hard to find a witch you can trust. If it were up to me, however, I'd probably trust Adele," said Clarice.

We walked into the main store, where Tyler sat with Bailey and Trixie.

"We're leaving," said Rebecca.

Tyler, who was eating pizza, sighed. "Can't we wait until we finish the food? I picked up four of these bad-boys and they won't be good reheated."

"No, we should leave now," said Clarice, looking troubled. "I'm quite certain that..."

Before she could finish, there was a flash of light and the room was filled with witches.

"You!" snarled Mark, stumbling towards me. "Did you think you could get away with it? Killing my mother?"

I stared at him in horror. "No, I didn't... it was the wand!"

My mother stepped in front of me and pointed at Mark. "Vivian's death was her own doing. Her greed and the darkness in her heart caused her fate."

Mark stared at Adrianne. "So, you're the sister, the one she wanted destroyed."

She raised her chin. "I'm her sister, yes."

He smiled evilly. "Well, then, I think it's only right that if you shared everything, including a birthday, that you share the same day of your death, as well."

Before anyone could react, he grabbed her hand and placed the wand into it.

Vivian's wand.

My mother's hand began to glow a bright red.

***

End of book one

Book Two, Enchanted Objects, now available.

Printed in Great Britain
by Amazon.co.uk, Ltd.,
Marston Gate.